Wyrde AND Wondrous

A HOUSE OF WERTH NOVEL

CHARLOTTE E. ENGLISH

CONTENTS

CHAPTER ONE

Winter passed reluctantly, that year; the chill, sunk deep into the bones of the earth, relinquished its grip slowly, and lingered late. But it did pass, and a bright, sun-drenched spring dawned upon the Werth family... at peace.

Peace. Can such a word apply to such a family? How does *peace* look, draped like a mantle over the shoulders of so strange a concoction of souls?

Well, peace meant Lord Werth left deceased Londoners undisturbed, abandoning necromantic antics in favour of the delights of books, afternoons in the parlour with his wife, and a good table at dinner. Peace meant Great-Aunt Honoria chiefly disported herself with Ivo Farthing, and largely blamelessly, fewer hair-raising pranks being played upon her nearest and dearest than usual. Peace meant Lady Werth, ice-free, devoted herself to the arranging of comforts across the townhouse as the weather warmed (once its singed roof had been repaired). And Theo? He abandoned theatres and gentlemen's clubs, at least for the time being, and closeted himself in the library.

What of the disastrous Gussie? This Honourable Miss Werth, having developed a taste for lurid romances, subscribed herself to a circulating library, and scarcely emerged for weeks.

Curious, is it not? One might even say, *suspicious.* So much apparent tranquillity could only be a façade, beneath which all manner of villainy must be plotting.

But one would be wrong. This was a true peace, a balmy interlude between house fires (twice); risen revenants (of unusual quantity, Great-Aunt Honoria excepted); homicidal literature (a certain amount of which might be taken in stride, but it had really become excessive); and nefarious-minded thespians (quite unusual indeed).

But if you are disposed to feel *concerned* by this; to wonder, perhaps, what on earth a Gussie Werth might be expected to do with herself through two or three tranquil months together; permit me to reassure you.

It didn't last.

ONE MORNING IN APRIL, Goodspeed found Gussie ensconced in the breakfast parlour with the second volume of *Melmoth the Wanderer.* The south-facing room enjoyed a great deal of sun on cloudless days (as this was); Gussie had caused a comfortable arm-chair to be placed for her in the best-favoured corner, and spent hours of every day tucked up in it. The only drawback to this regularity of habit was its predictability; she was altogether too easy to find, and thus to interrupt.

Goodspeed's entry and discreet cough prompted a fair scowl of annoyance, an expression Gussie quickly suppressed. To do him credit, the new butler never interposed his presence without a good reason.

'What is it, Goodspeed?' said she, inserting a finger between the pages of her book to keep her place.

Goodspeed made a half-bow, and proffered something wrapped in brown paper. 'A package was left for you, Miss Werth.'

'A package?' This was most unusual, and Gussie's curiosity was immediately roused. 'Left where, pray?'

'On the front doorstep, Miss. Gabriel discovered it not five minutes ago.'

Gabriel was a footman, and until recently he would in all likelihood have brought such a parcel straight to Gussie herself. Since the advent of Goodspeed, however, things had changed in the household. Every one of the servants had quickly come to rely heavily on Mr Cornelius Goodspeed; they consulted him in everything, and deferred to him in everything.

This troubled the family not at all, for their own attitude towards their new butler was scarcely any different. Goodspeed had talents.

'How curious,' said Gussie, taking the package. 'Thank you, Goodspeed. Shall you remain while I open it?'

'I would be interested to learn of the contents, Miss.'

Gussie accepted this with a nod, and tore into the package. It had not travelled far, she judged, for it was but loosely wrapped, and the paper remained crisp and undamaged.

Inside it, she discovered a book. No aged and weighty tome, this, for it was barely the size of her own hand. Bound in lavender kid, soft as butter, and with a silk ribbon bookmark in a matching hue, the book was patently a lady's journal, or something of that nature. A pretty thing, and innocuous, but nonetheless, upon beholding it, Gussie felt a chill of apprehension.

Nonsense, she scolded herself. She had grown wary of mysterious books, that was all, and it was no wonder.

The pages were blank.

'I believe I am intended to write in it,' Gussie said, looking up at Goodspeed. 'I never was much in the habit of keeping a diary, I confess.'

She handed the little volume to the butler, who examined it carefully. 'Have you no ideas as to who might have sent it?'

'Not one. I am not in possession of the sorts of friends who might gift me with such an object. And if I were, I can only imagine they would hand it to me directly, not wrap it up in paper and leave it on the doorstep, without a note.'

'It is peculiar,' Goodspeed agreed, returning the book to her. Both eyed the diary warily, in case it should take it upon itself to engage in some troublesome antic. It didn't, however.

'I shall keep it,' Gussie decided. 'Perhaps an answer to this little mystery will present itself, in due time.'

'I believe it must,' Goodspeed agreed. 'Whoever sent it must have done so for a purpose.'

With which wisdom, he bowed and withdrew, returning, no doubt, to his daily task of directing and managing every aspect of the Werth family's London life.

Gussie turned the diary over in her hands, musing. It was not quite impossible that Clarissa had sent it; she did take odd notions into her head, sometimes.

Regretfully, Gussie laid aside the second volume of *Melmoth the Wanderer* and abandoned her sunny arm-chair. She had not seen Clarissa for some days, and a visit would likely be welcome.

And besides, she would soon be in urgent need of volume three.

'If I wanted to leave you mysterious literature I would send something salacious,' Clarissa declared, an hour later. '*The Monk*, perhaps, or that shocking new romance everyone is talking of.'

'That is what I thought,' Gussie agreed, returning the diary to her reticule. 'But I considered it worth the enquiry.'

She had found Clarissa (eventually) in the kitchens of the Selwyn townhouse, engaged in making jellies. Quite *why* she was making jellies when Lord Maundevyle employed an excellent cook was beyond anybody to explain — including, in all likelihood, Clarissa. Some freak had seized her after breakfast, and here she was, three hours later, up to her elbows in calves' feet and fruit.

'I cannot see why an empty book should excite such interest,' Clarissa declared, returning her attention to the repellently fragrant mess she was making. 'And it is such an insipid colour, too.'

'I should give it no thought whatsoever, except for the manner of its delivery,' Gussie agreed. 'Left especially for me, and anonymously.'

'That is more intriguing.' Clarissa did not appear much intrigued, being wholly engrossed in her culinary escapade. 'I believe Henry is at home,' she added, with a sidelong smirk in Gussie's direction. 'He will be enthralled to hear of it, I'm sure.'

'I am not going to marry Lord Maundevyle,' Gussie said promptly, and rather by rote. She had been obliged to repeat it several times already.

'Of course you are not,' Clarissa agreed serenely. 'You are merely going to favour him with your company while you pursue the mystery of this curious book.'

'I shall do exactly that.' Disgusted by the aromas circulating in the kitchen, Gussie withdrew.

HENRY WAS OFTEN TO be found in the best parlour, engaged in a book, and thither Gussie went first.

To her surprise, though someone occupied Henry's usual seat at the mahogany table, it was not Lord Maundevyle.

'Mr. Selwyn,' said she, making her curtsey. 'Forgive my intrusion. I was sent by your sister in search of your brother.'

Charles looked up from the book spread before him. Once, he would have regarded Gussie with undisguised ill-feeling, or — at best — a kind of sardonic mockery. Since the Werths had extricated both he and Lord Maundevyle from a dangerous scrape, that ill-feeling had faded.

Not that he had arrived, yet, at anything like congeniality. Merely a blank neutrality, most of the time, and a civil manner. Gussie found this more than acceptable.

'I am afraid you are to be disappointed,' said Charles, politely enough. 'Henry has gone out.'

'What a pity.' Gussie considered, and withdrew the journal from her reticule anyway. 'I received this in a parcel, only this morning, and I was hoping to ask him about it.'

'You believe that Henry might have sent it to you?' Charles regarded the little lavender diary with a slight frown.

'I think it most unlikely, but I may be wrong.'

Charles met Gussie's gaze, briefly, before returning to his book. 'While I can believe him capable of offering gifts, Miss Werth, I do not imagine he would have made so mundane a choice for you. And since the purpose of a gift, in such a context, is to win favour, I do not see why he would have been so clandestine about it either.' He turned a page.

Since these thoughts echoed Gussie's own, she did not dispute them. Nor did she reply to the implication that Lord Maundevyle might be disposed to offer her some manner of courting-gift. 'If you should hear of anything that may prove relevant to my little mystery, I would be obliged if you would share it,' was all that she said.

'Certainly.' Charles did not look up from his reading, and Gussie thought it best to withdraw.

That the disdainful, somewhat wastrel Charles Selwyn should turn bookish seemed almost impossible, but stranger things had certainly happened. Gussie knew that Miss Frostell was, in part, responsible for this curious change; she had guided Charles out of a deep affliction through her gentle reading of gentle books, and it seemed the habit had persisted with him.

All in all, his recent trials had immeasurably improved him. Gussie put it down as an important lesson: torment could occasionally be excellent for both health and character, a reflection which pleased her rather more than it ought.

She did not hazard her luck with Lady Maundevyle. That lady, always capricious in the extreme, veered wildly from strong approval to deep resentment towards the Werths, and Gussie found the experience trying. She left the house instead, and hesitated for some moments on the street.

She *could* pursue the matter of the diary further. Someone had to have made the little book, and, it being a neat, clean job, it was most likely professionally bound. There were many bookbinders across London, no doubt, and a few enquiries might soon turn up a clue as to where the book had come from.

But the errand would be wearisome, and as like as not to turn up nothing at all. A desultory rain pattered over Gussie's bonnet and pelisse, aiding her inclination to give up the point altogether. After all, she had no reason to imagine the book possessed any especial significance. It was only a collection of pages, and had done nothing to excite such interest.

She turned her steps instead in the direction of Hambly's Circulating Library; Mrs. Hambly would have something new for her by today, and *Melmoth the Wanderer* would not last her beyond the evening.

Gussie's errands began and ended, then, with books, be it journals or novels; but the latter proved of a vastly more absorbing nature than the former.

At least for the present.

CHAPTER TWO

LORD BEDGBERRY MAY HAVE given up the dubious delights of gambling, drinking and womanising, but the glories of possessing his own gentleman's quarters proved longer-lasting.

Not that he had troubled to discuss the matter with his mother and father, let alone Gussie. He merely failed to come home of an evening, once in a while, and fondly imagined his activities a mystery. A certain sardonic look from Gussie had long since punctured this airy illusion, but Theo maintained the pretence anyway; for some reason, it rather entertained him.

The apartments chiefly housed his collection of texts, including those borrowed from two or three subscription libraries of which he had become a member. Such an excess of bookishness to strike the Werths and Selwyns alike, is it not? One might imagine them all reformed characters, if one were feeling particularly optimistic.

We join Theo at precisely the moment this blameless existence became, once again, *interesting*.

In other words, the moment when, upon returning to these scholarly quarters with a fresh armload of books, he discovered a new addition lying upon the doorstep. A small volume, wrapped neatly in brown paper; he caught it up and carried it in with the rest of his acquisitions, imagining some bookseller to have left it for him.

Only once the paper was torn away did he discover his error. The book, leather-bound in claret red, was blank inside, which declared it to be some manner of journal. Which was absurd. Whoever heard of a gentleman keeping a diary, like a lady?

Perhaps it might be intended for him to record scientific findings, or notes upon his travels abroad, were Theo inclined towards either pursuit. But though he enjoyed reading about other people's scientific endeavours, he had not the patience to conduct such investigations himself. And as for travel, he had had quite enough of that for the time being.

He turned over both book and wrapping paper, seeking some clue as to the sender, but discovered none. Not even his address, printed upon the exterior. Perhaps it had been intended for someone else, and left at his doorstep in error?

He wrapped it back up again, and left it outside his door. If it were a mistake, whoever had left it might soon realise their error, and return for it.

Having performed which neighbourly act, he returned to his reading and promptly forgot about it.

But the next day, it was still there.

And the next, and the next.

At length, Theo abandoned his expectation that somebody might take the thing away, and brought it back inside. He awarded it a station upon a mahogany console table near one of his long windows, where it lay untouched, forgotten again.

At least for the present.

'GREAT-UNCLE SILVESTER?' THEO EXCLAIMED, on the fourth morning after the delivery of the mysterious journal. 'What are you doing here?'

He had wandered into his apartments, half distracted as usual; he had but just acquired a new text on the intricacies of necromancy from the library, and was already four pages in. As such, he did not immediately see the cathedral grotesque hunched atop the back of his preferred chair. It was the grinding sound of ancient stone that alerted him; Silvester's idea of laughter, he had once concluded, but it was difficult to be sure.

The grotesque flapped his wings at his great-grand-nephew, and took to the air. 'Shouldn't wonder at it if it should rain later,' he remarked in gravelly tones, and landed, a little awkwardly, atop a certain mahogany console table.

It took Theo a moment to notice that the table was, other than the grotesque, empty.

'I say, have you moved my book?' Theo turned about, and searched the room until he discovered it lying atop a half-book-case under a window. Silvester had added it to a stack of volumes of similar size, if not similar character; unusually neat, for him. 'I suppose this is a better spot for it, to be sure,' Theo added.

Silvester nodded his granite head up and down, and chuckled. 'A fine filly,' he pronounced. Theo could not tell whether he intended the remark to refer to a horse or a woman, and decided not to ask.

'Well, and you have found out my secret abode,' said Theo. 'I am not best pleased about it, I'll own. You won't tell the others, will you?'

'A spot of trout-fishing would be very pleasant,' answered Great-Uncle Silvester.

'Thank you. Not that I imagine they will be much disturbed by it, but a man has to have a secret or two, no?' He frowned, and added, 'Come to think of it, how did you find me out? Did you follow me from the house?'

Silvester only cackled.

It was the sort of thing Gussie would do, Theo thought darkly. Perhaps she had done so long since; that would explain the acerbic comments she had once or twice levelled at him, whenever he had talked airily (and mendaciously) of an evening spent with Hargreve at the club.

'Gussie told you, didn't she?' he groaned. 'Probably told everybody.' He sighed, and sank into the chair recently vacated by the grotesque. He could not have said why the idea displeased him; why should he prefer for his family to imagine him out carousing, rather than reading?

The winter's escapade with that *actress*. That was what had done the mischief. It had shaken Theo more than he cared to admit; it did not seem quite the *thing* to be so overset by a conniving woman, no matter how clever she had proved to be. Or how oblivious *he* had proved himself to be.

No, let them all imagine him unfazed — if Gussie would hold her tongue, at any rate. Perhaps he would speak to her—

'Silvester,' he said abruptly. 'Did you move the book *again*?' For he had been gazing absently out of the very window beneath which the new, claret-bound book had recently lain, and it was not there now.

But he hadn't seen — or heard — Silvester move.

A tendril of unease sent him out of his chair, and striding about the room. There it was — on the back of his chair. The chair in which he'd been sitting.

'Not very amusing, Uncle,' he said severely. 'You'll give me quite a fright.'

Great-Uncle Silvester creaked and groaned and cackled to himself, shifting his feet restlessly atop the console table. 'Wretched weather,' he declared. 'And I would not dance with him if he were to ask me.'

Not for the first time, Theo wished his uncle might contrive to express himself with greater clarity. 'You did move the book, I suppose?' he said uneasily. 'Only you managed the business so neatly I did not happen to catch you at it...'

Silvester was shaking his head. Finding this insufficient, he launched himself into the air with enough force to leave the table rocking wildly beneath him, and flapped over to the chair.

Once perched thereupon, he lifted a granite foot and unceremoniously kicked the book onto the floor.

A few victorious hops celebrated this achievement, and he took up cackling again.

'I suppose that's clear enough,' murmured Theo, staring at the felled book in mounting horror. Great-Uncle Silvester had not moved the book. Then who had?

Or *what*?

'The thing moved itself, didn't it?' he said, turning cold with dismay. Horror of horrors. They had but just got rid of the ancient and malevolent Book of Werth, *and* the additional monster Gussie had saddled them with. At great cost to the estate, no less! And now, here was another maleficent volume turned up to taunt them.

'Though,' he said aloud, struck by a new thought. 'Perhaps it is not like the other Books, after all. Perhaps it is merely haunted!' In the same way that the ghostly remains of Great-Uncle Silvester haunted the cathedral grotesque, and caused it to flap itself about almost as though it were living.

Why a spirit would choose to haunt a book, of all things, Theo could not guess; the choice seemed an odd one. But who was he to quarrel with the logic of ghosts? He had never sampled the state, himself (not yet).

He found the prospect of a haunting by person or persons unknown so immensely reassuring that he decided to adopt it as a certainty. 'Friend of yours, perhaps?' he said to Silvester, picking up the book.

That did not quite make sense; if the book had wanted to seek out Silvester, surely it would have delivered itself to the Werths' townhouse, not to Theo's lodgings. But this discrepancy would surely be explained in due time.

Theo took the book outside again, and propped it up against the door frame. 'I should go elsewhere, if I were you,' he informed it. 'Not very lively in these parts, you know.'

Firmly shutting the door on it, Theo turned back to his books. Great-Uncle Silvester was cackling again, more raucously than ever, but that didn't mean anything, surely? He was always giggling away about something or other.

Theo put the matter out of his mind, settled himself with his new book on *The Care and Preservation of Corpses Raised From the Grave*, and began, once again, to read.

28TH APRIL 1821

The Personal Diary of Miss Augusta Werth, First Entry

I cannot explain what sudden freak should have seized me, that I find myself keeping a diary. Perhaps it is merely the suggestive powers of having a blank and handsome volume close at hand for the purpose, a circumstance hitherto unknown to me. Or perhaps it has somewhat to do with social pressures — lowering thought. I do not find myself in company with young ladies of my own station very often, but when I do, the conversation cannot help but turn upon the twin delights of delicious gossip and the recording thereof, be it in letters to one's acquaintance or in one's own diary.

The tendency of diaries to prove sadly mundane being a universal constant, no effort should be spared to make them as sensational as possible. What, then, shall I write in mine? What is sensational to the majority is mundane to us. Having missed my opportunity to record all the electrifying events of the past year — attempted murders, irate dragons, resurrected ancestors, house fires, villainous plots, and social opprobrium aplenty — I take up my diary at a time of peace and quiet. Must I then fabricate some salacious event?

No. I am, at heart, a truthful person, and there can be little entertainment in lies. I must focus, then, upon the only truly strange event in recent months, that being: the appearance of this little book (unexplained) and my curious urge to write in its pages.

I have, as yet, no real clues to elucidate either happenstance. I trust that this will change.

So wrote Gussie one cool evening, seated in her bed-chamber with a warm shawl wrapped over her shoulders and her hair in curl papers. She found the experience more satisfying than otherwise, and closed the book's lavender covers with a sense of having accomplished something, however minor.

She even took the book to bed with her, and laid it upon a side-table as she slept.

The following morning brought her material for a further entry, for Mr. Ballantine came to call. He knew the habits of the family well enough by now, and timed his visit perfectly. No sooner had Lord and Lady Werth finished their (rather late) breakfast than the front door knocker sounded.

Goodspeed soon appeared at the door of the breakfast parlour. 'I have admitted Mr. Ballantine, milord. Milady. Miss. He is in the drawing-room.'

'Delightful,' pronounced Lady Werth, rising from the breakfast table at once. 'Who is he here to see, Goodspeed?'

'I understand he would like to see you all. I have already informed him that Lord Bedgberry is from home at present.'

Nothing would have persuaded Gussie to miss an audience with Hugh Ballantine, so she received this news with approval. 'Theo will have to catch up later,' she said, following her aunt and uncle to the door. 'Perhaps that will teach him not to spend so much time *carousing*.' She smirked.

'Theo may wish to set up his own establishment, sometime soon,' said Lord Werth. 'I know you will miss him, Gussie, but I am afraid you will have to accept it, whenever he does.'

Gussie was too much disconcerted to reply. Theo, with an independent establishment? Perish the thought.

The idea that she would miss him she dismissed with an inward snort. Stuff and nonsense.

Further reflections on this interesting prospect would have to wait, for they were arrived at the drawing-room, and Mr. Ballantine was on his feet and bowing politely to his distant cousins. 'I hope I have not intruded too early,' he was saying. 'I come on an errand of some importance.'

Lord and Lady Werth both looked, instantly and jointly, at Gussie. Their expressions registered a mixture of apprehension and resignation, which made Gussie feel very indignant indeed. 'I haven't done anything,' she protested.

Ballantine's mouth twitched. 'On this occasion, indeed, it is no escapade of Miss Werth's I come to discuss.'

'Thank you,' said Gussie primly, and sat down, folding her hands neatly in her lap.

'At least, no past escapade,' the Runner amended. 'I might, perhaps, hope to inspire a future one.'

Gussie brightened. 'You have *my* attention,' she informed him.

Her aunt and uncle developed a wary demeanour. 'You had better tell us all about it,' said Lord Werth. 'Spare no details, if you please.'

Ballantine took a chair. He was looking a little grim, Gussie thought, but that was not unusual. At least he was properly human-shaped, today, and not wearing his much more alarming ogre form. 'Perhaps you have already heard something of the business at hand,' he began. 'There has been a series of thefts, I'm afraid. Jewels, primarily. Family heirlooms, that kind of thing. And all taken from Wyrded families among the gentry and nobility.'

Gussie felt immediately alert. Despite her periodic exposure to the tittering gossip of the city, she had heard no such thing. A glance at her aunt and uncle revealed a similar ignorance; they both looked blank, and surprised. 'Is this widely known?' she asked.

'I see that it isn't,' answered Ballantine. 'It is a source of some embarrassment, perhaps, to lose such precious possessions as that. The families in question may not like to make the matter public.'

'Which families?' asked Lady Werth.

'I have received reports from Mrs. White, Lady Goulding, Mr. Windham, the Misses Sherbourne, and Lady Ashenhurst. The items taken were chiefly diamonds, emeralds and sapphires — necklaces and head-pieces, a cravat pin, and one brooch. Items one wears to the grander sort of public event, in short, and indeed, all of the jewels were noticed missing either during or shortly after their owner's attendance at a ball.'

Those same balls Lord and Lady Werth usually chose not to attend, and which, therefore, Gussie had not experienced either. Perhaps they were right, and she would find it all an intolerable crush. And perhaps they were also right that to turn Gussie loose among so many people, Wyrded or otherwise, would prove disastrous.

Still, she would like a chance to find out.

'How unfortunate,' murmured Lady Werth, perhaps reflecting with satisfaction on the safety of her own excellent diamonds. 'While I sympathise with the plight of the Whites, the Windhams and so on, I am not yet understanding what this has to do with Gussie.'

Mr. Ballantine hesitated, a sign one might interpret as either worrying (if one were Lady Werth) or highly promising (if one were Gussie). 'The fact is, I am having some difficulty investigating these thefts,' he finally began. 'The fact that they exclusively occur at events open only to those of great wealth and high status is a barrier to me, and to my men. I cannot make any appearance at these balls myself, or not openly. I would welcome some assistance from those who can.'

Gussie's heart leapt. 'Yes!' she said at once. 'I would be delighted to assist you, Mr. Ballantine.'

'Gussie,' said Lord Werth, warningly. 'Pray remember that you have not yet been given leave.'

'Oh, but you won't deny me, surely?' She smiled hopefully upon her aunt and uncle in turn. 'It is high time I began to be *seen* by our excellent and Wyrded peers, unless you would like to be saddled with me forever. And I shall only be there to observe, you know, and to listen to the gossip.'

Lord and Lady Werth merely looked at her, scepticism patent upon both their faces.

Ballantine gave a slight cough. 'It is my hope that all three of you might be persuaded to assist,' he elaborated. 'So she will remain under your watchful eye, Lord Werth.'

'And Theo, too,' Gussie put in. 'He and all his eligibility shall be paraded before every Wyrded and unwed lady in London! How he shall detest it.' The thought made her smile.

'What precisely would you like us to do?' said Lady Werth, transferring her forbidding gaze to Ballantine.

'As Miss Werth says, watch and listen. Besides that, I leave it to you to determine how your combined Wyrded arts might best be employed.'

'Do you wish us to catch this thief in the act?'

'Should you be presented with an opportunity to do so, by all means. But no. It is information I need, in order to identify the culprit. After that, I shall be quite capable of apprehending this person myself.'

Mr. Ballantine's speech always became especially correct when addressing Lord and Lady Werth, Gussie had previously noticed. Especially if he happened to be petitioning them for something.

Gussie herself knew when to stop talking. She instead chose to direct her most beseeching look at her aunt and uncle, and adopted a pose she hoped looked particularly respectable and trustworthy. Difficult qualities to convey by posture alone, but something must have worked, for Lady Werth relented.

'I am not opposed to attending one or two functions,' she decided. 'And we will see what we shall see.'

Gussie crowed with delight. 'I have been so *bored*,' she confided. 'Nothing has happened since Lord Maundevyle set the roof on fire! How intolerably dull it has been.'

'The roof, however, appreciates the interval,' answered Lord Werth dryly. 'Being now again in one piece.'

Lord Maundevyle hadn't called since the episode in question. Gussie thought it cowardly of him, though more probably it was the consequence of profound embarrassment and a degree of guilt. He could not be talked out of either, despite the fact that he had been acting under mesmerism, and not at all himself. He had assuaged his feelings somewhat by paying for the roof repairs, but he continued to absent himself.

Gussie found it unaccountable.

'I am delighted to hear it,' Ballantine said, and he actually smiled. 'Thank you. Please be aware that I, or one of my men, shall be near at hand whenever you are at work, if not in the ballroom itself. Your safety, and that of Lord Bedgberry, are a very high priority.'

Gussie perceived that Theo was not to be given a choice in the matter, a fact of which she approved. It was always best not to give Theo an opportunity to be difficult, or he most assuredly *would*.

She clapped her hands in delight, and descended from her dignity so far as to bounce a little in her seat. 'What felicity! I feel like a new woman already.'

Mr. Ballantine's expression of slightly sick apprehension spoke of some dawning regret, but it was too late for that now. Gussie smiled graciously upon him. 'Don't worry, Mr. Ballantine. I shall be on my very best behaviour, I assure you.'

'I believe that may be what I am worried about,' he muttered in reply.

CHAPTER THREE

Chesterton notes that "decay is a sordid business; the chief enemy of every revenant, save, perhaps, those whose lack of vanity precludes any interest in their personal appearance. Instances have been recorded of an undead individual reduced to nought but sinew and bone without suffering any material diminishment in range of movement, &c, but such a person must resign themselves to a solitary existence after death, for the visage being in every respect horrific and alarming, they are unlikely to enjoy any particular acquaintance thereafter."

Wonder how Great-Aunt Honoria manages the business. She retains not only a passable enough visage — skin, eyeballs and whatnot — but even has something of a coiffure. But, she is not Raised from the grave, in the way of my father's arts. More of an apparition than a physical body, I am like to think, but have not investigated. May enquire. Ivo as well.

Must say that Chesterton's prospect appeals. Were I nothing but "Sinew and Bone", even Gussie could not wish to pester me any further. Surely? And there would never again be any talk of marriage.

I am still alive, of course, the state being a material impediment to so happy a condition. Perhaps later.

These notes, hastily scrawled in Theo's careless handwriting, and blotted in one or two places, afforded him both considerable satisfaction and some puzzlement upon later perusal. He could not have said whence came the urge to record these passing ideas; nor how the claret-coloured book, safely stationed outside the door (as it had been, he remembered that very clearly) had contrived not only to wend its way indoors once again, but also to station itself at his elbow just when he had wanted to jot these few things down.

The entry was made before he was aware. He did not feel unhappy with it, all things considered.

'Well, and if you are to make yourself useful, I suppose you may stay,' Theo informed the book, and let it rest upon the arm of his sofa. 'Just mind that you don't wander off when I want you,' he warned it. 'Or I shall throw you into the fire.'

The book made no answer. If it were a haunt, like Great-Uncle Silvester's grotesque, then he might expect it to possess some power of speech, but it had yet to manifest anything of the kind. Still, perhaps it was shy. He had not been very welcoming to it, at first, and anybody of even ordinary sensibility might feel abashed by such treatment.

He ought not threaten it with the fire, that being so, but it was too late to think of that now.

When he made his return to the family townhouse later that morning, he took the little book with him, tucked into a pocket of his coat. His feelings towards it were undergoing so swift a change, he felt comforted by its presence; like having a friend along with him, one in whom he could confide.

He entered his home via the servants' entrance at the rear, as was his wont when he hoped to escape notice, and retreat to his room — or the library — unobserved.

He was not to be so fortunate. The household being in an unusually lively state, Theo soon collected that something had happened.

'What on earth's afoot?' Theo asked of Goodspeed, whom he had encountered in the passage leading from the kitchen down to the butler's pantry. His mother's lady's maid had but just whisked past him, in a state of high excitement, and he could hear some manner of tumult emanating from upstairs.

Goodspeed bowed. 'Good morning, Lord Bedgberry. You find us in a state of happy preparation.'

'That sounds ominous.'

Goodspeed was too scrupulously correct in his manners to smile at such a comment. 'Indeed, sir,' he agreed. 'Mr. Ballantine has called.'

'That sounds *very* ominous.'

'Perhaps, sir. I shall not forestall your lady mother, for I am sure she would wish to share the news with you herself.'

'You couldn't just give me a hint?' Theo pleaded. 'Only tell me it isn't anything of Gussie's doing, at least? I believe I could bear anything, but that.'

'I should be sorry to disappoint so natural a wish, sir,' said Goodspeed, confirming Theo's worst fears, and neatly leaving it to Lady Werth to dash her son's dearest hopes.

Theo sighed. 'No doubt she's in high gig,' he grumbled. 'Ballantine ought to know better.' He did not specify *what* Ballantine ought to know better, merely took himself upstairs with feelings of grave foreboding and no little exasperation.

He found his mother in the best parlour, seated at the elegant new mahogany table with a quantity of letters before her. Letters — and calling cards, not to mention articles that resembled invitations.

'Mama?' said Theo, finding his entrance unobserved.

Lady Werth looked up, and surveyed him critically. 'That won't do,' she decided. 'You had better have a regular valet, Theo, if we are to make an entrance into polite society.'

'We're to do what?'

'In such cases as these, appearance is everything. And considering the uncertain reputation enjoyed by our family, we had better employ every possible advantage.'

'We're to *what*?' Theo said again.

'Jewels, Theo,' said his mother, returning to her letters. 'Stolen jewels, from several families of station, wealth and Wyrde, and Mr. Ballantine beseeches our aid in determining the culprit.'

Theo's head whirled. 'We're going to balls,' he realised, and swiftly on the heels of that depressing realisation: 'This *is* Gussie's doing, isn't it? All because she wants to be a Bow-Street Runner, of all things.'

'I imagine so,' said Lady Werth serenely, penning something in emphatic black ink.

'Well, I shan't object to anything Gussie wants to do, if she *must* be so eccentric,' said Theo, magnanimously, and somewhat mendaciously. 'Only I don't see why I should have to go, too.'

'There may be gentlemen involved in the thievery, and your father will want your assistance in finding it out.'

'Papa is mixed up in this nonsense, too?' Theo was incredulous.

'I have felt for some time that we have become too reclusive,' was Lady Werth's reply. 'Here is a sound reason to enlarge our acquaintance, and see a little of the world.'

This being very much his mother's style of reasoning, Theo concluded gloomily that Lord Werth had been *managed*, probably by his mother and Gussie both.

And so was he to be. Any hopes of enlisting his father's support in resisting the unstoppable tide of Lady Werth and Miss Werth, united in a mission, faded.

'I would much rather read,' he informed his mother, with a note of desperation.

'And I would much rather go home, but somebody burnt down half of our family estate. Such a pity.' She did not so much as look at Theo as she said it, but he felt the full weight of her meaning regardless.

He had not been fully responsible for the burning of Werth Towers, but the disaster had happened on his watch, and he was not yet entirely forgiven.

Masterful manoeuvring, he thought sourly.

'Very well,' he muttered. 'I will attend a ball, if I must. Only do not make me pay morning calls, if you please.'

Lady Werth's only response to this being a brief, forbidding glance, Theo slunk away, defeated.

THE NEW VALET PROVED to be no idle threat. How Lady Werth had contrived to identify, interview and recruit a suitable person so quickly was beyond Theo's imagination to account for, save for the horrible suspicion that she had been planning the move for some time.

More likely it was Goodspeed's doing. Theo curbed his (very natural) resentment as best he could, particularly when the butler was so good as to introduce to him the new keeper of his attire.

'Victor Daundelyon,' announced Goodspeed, having brought the offending person to Theo's notice in the library, shortly before dinner. 'He comes highly recommended, my lord, and I trust you will find in him a valet of considerable skill.'

Theo bestowed a careless, and only slightly forbidding, glance upon his unwanted lackey, and found him uninspiring to behold. A tall, spare fellow several years older than Theo himself, he judged, he had neat brown hair, stern features, impeccable attire, and a level gaze. Indeed, he seemed scarcely deferential at all, returning Theo's look stare for stare, except for when he made his duty bow. This pleased Theo rather more than he might have expected.

'Yes, well,' said Theo, vaguely waving a hand in what was probably intended as a dismissal.

Goodspeed cleared his throat. 'I believe the dinner gong will shortly sound, sir?'

'I daresay,' Theo replied, returning to his book.

'Your lady mother will perhaps wish to see you properly turned out, sir?'

Theo saw Goodspeed's point at once. Having provided him with a valet, she would wish to see him make use of the fellow immediately, no doubt wishful of inspecting the results prior to his presentation before half of London society. The Wyrde half.

He briefly weighed the relative inconvenience of permitting this Daundelyon to truss him up and strut him about like a turkey, versus having to explain over the soup-tureen why he had instead appeared in his ordinary state of disorder.

'Very well,' he sighed, and rose from his very comfortable nook. 'You may go, Goodspeed.'

The butler bowed and withdrew, accepting this mild rebuke without comment.

Daundelyon occupied himself with surveying Theo's attire. He appeared unimpressed, but that may be the customary set of his features.

Theo fingered his coat with a suppressed sigh. It was the dark green one, his favourite. 'You aren't to do anything *permanent* to this, understand? It is a coat I favour above every other.'

Daundelyon bowed. 'Your lordship won't wish to wear it in to dinner, I daresay? I'll take it in hand, my lord, while you dine.' He spoke rather softly, with a lilt to his words that put Theo in mind of Miss Frostell's mode of speech.

'And what might that entail?' Theo demanded, rather afeared for his coat. It was well worn-in, easy to shrug himself in and out of. What's more, it had good, deep pockets, for the storing of books. Including the little claret-coloured journal.

'Only a little maintenance, sir. Those elbows will want a stitch or two in them, I shouldn't wonder, and a good brush-up wouldn't hurt it at all.'

Theo began to feel that this valeting business might not be so bad after all, a brightening of spirits he was soon to regret; for the arranging of his hair, the complex knotting of his cravat, and the squeezing of his shoulders into a much tighter coat, all left him feeling very cross.

He was rewarded upon his entrance at dinner, whereupon his lady mother's face registered approval and surprise in equal measure. 'Delightful, Theo,' she said, gracious in victory.

'Well, cousin, and I should hardly know you,' came Gussie's inevitable sally, which he ignored.

Lord Werth said nothing, only met his son's gaze with a brief, wry look. Great-Aunt Honoria was nowhere in evidence, presumably still swanning about up in the eaves with her *caro sposo*.

That left Miss Frostell, who ordinarily would not have ventured an opinion. Today, though, she surprised him as he took his seat by saying: 'My, has not Victor excelled himself! What an honour it is for him, I am sure.'

Theo found it impossible to comprehend this speech. 'You are in some manner acquainted with my valet, Miss Frostell?'

'Oh! To be sure. My sister's son, he is. She married Mr. Daundelyon straight out of the school-room,' she said — (pronouncing "Daundelyon" similarly to "dandelion") — 'and it *was* said that she was too young at the time. But a happy marriage it's been, sir, as I'm sure you'll be glad to know, though there never was a great deal of money between them. Poor Victor does them great credit, however. He was valet to a baron, you know, some four or five years.'

'I am sure he will prove an excellent addition to our staff,' said Lady Werth. 'I am most grateful to our excellent Goodspeed for thinking of him.'

'So am I, my lady, and I shall be sure to tell my sister you said so,' promised Miss Frostell.

'What a happy family party we are becoming,' Gussie observed. 'I must set eyes on this excellent Mr. Daundelyon myself, if he is a relative of yours, Frosty.'

'No doubt you'll encounter him soon enough,' muttered Theo. 'He will be here, I believe, every day.'

'And am I to have a maid as well, Aunt? I think poor Hayton will think herself very ill-used, though, if I am.'

Theo contrived, after a moment, to remember that Hayton was the name of his mother's lady's maid, an unassuming woman of middle years who had been taken on after the roof fire. Probably she had the arranging of Gussie's hair, too, matters which interested him so little, he permitted his attention to wander away from the conversation entirely.

He was roused during the first remove by Gussie's saying, in a penetrating tone, 'What is that book, Theo? It doesn't look like your customary reading material.'

He glanced up, momentarily puzzled. He had not been reading, having been soundly banned from bringing books into the dining-room long ago (to his great, and enduring, disappointment).

It was the claret-coloured journal, of course, sitting meekly at his elbow, quite as though he had placed it there himself.

'Oh, just a little thing I write a few notes into,' he said, returning it to his pocket once more. The pockets, in fact, were not very good in this dinner-coat, and the book might simply have fallen out, save that it would most likely have ended up on the floor.

Gussie did not immediately reply. Theo found this so unexpected, his cousin rarely being at a loss for a rapid rejoinder, that he cast a searching look at her face, still turned towards him.

He found her gazing in similar spirit at *him*. 'A recent purchase, I collect?' she finally said.

Theo found himself curiously unwilling to explain quite how he had come by the book — or, more accurately, how the book had come by him. So he answered only with a noncommittal noise, and the subject dropped.

CHAPTER
FOUR

Let this be a lesson worthy of remembering: anything you may wish to do, be it ever so unlikely, you have only to be firm, and unwavering, and you are sure of one day carrying your point.

Was it not Mr. Ballantine himself who refused me as a colleague? And now, to come entreating my assistance! Forced to own that there are instances where a woman, and indeed a woman of rank, can be of great use to him in his enquiries. I am very well pleased.

The case may not be quite so exciting as last time — no murders or high danger, alas — but one must begin somewhere. I am confident of our soon apprehending the thief, and having done so, Mr. Ballantine will have no cause to deny me further involvement with the business of Bow Street.

Our first escapade is to take place tomorrow night, my aunt having discovered among her oft-neglected correspondence an in-

vitation to an evening party at the house of Lady Alicia Greaves. Our appearance must occasion some surprise, for it is the first such engagement we shall have attended since our arrival in London. Which means, of course, that it is the first such occasion for me, in the whole of my life! I have promised my aunt not to Wyrde anyone, which means I must keep my hands largely to myself; though I shall wear my pale yellow gloves, of course, and perhaps that will be sufficient.

The hour of the party arrived, and found Gussie in the highest of spirits. All things considered, she was not at all without inclination for an evening of pleasant conversation and fine music; and since Hayton had put her into a delightful gown of ivory silk, and put up her dark locks into an elaborate and fetching style, she felt that she looked well, and should not mind being very much stared at.

She had, perforce, to remind herself of the true purpose of the evening's entertainment, so carried away was she with enjoyment.

They were announced, upon arrival — 'Lord and Lady Werth; Lord Bedgberry; Miss Werth' — in a manner rather grand, and their appearance caused a stir. Conversation all but halted, until the other guests had looked their fill at these oddities: a gaggle of Werths abroad, nicely dressed, and on their very best behaviour.

The house of Lady Alicia being grand, and the family (apparently) wealthy, the drawing-room into which they were conducted was sumptuous, and furnished in the latest styles.

The hues were pale blue and sea-green; the materials silk and mahogany; the light dazzling, due to a shocking quantity of beeswax candles. Every chair and chaise longue bore an elegantly lounging occupant, a bouquet of ladies and gentlemen in satins and silks.

More than one quizzing-glass or lorgnette was turned towards the Werths.

Gussie saw no one that she knew. She did not believe her aunt and uncle were much acquainted with the gathering, either; the invitation had been sent on account of some trivial tie between the two families long before, offered as a matter of course, or habit, and never with any expectation of its being accepted.

Lady Alicia recovered first, and rose to welcome her guests. A woman of Lady Werth's general age, she was stout and smiling in rose-coloured damask. Her cheeks flushed as pink as her gown and her eyes sparkled as she received Lord and Lady Werth, and Theo, and finally Gussie herself.

Gussie found her hands taken, and pressed, and a beaming look of gladness directed at her.

She withdrew her hands as soon as she could, without giving offence; — 'Perhaps, ma'am, you have not heard tell of the nature of my Wyrde, but it is judged best not to maintain contact with me for very long' — a revelation laughed away, for, as Lady Alicia immediately said, 'Oh, as to that! We are every one of us Wyrded already, are not we? No, no, indeed, there is not one of us without some ghoulish eccentricity' — and she laughed very heartily at the reflection.

Gussie felt much relieved, being thus freed to mingle as she chose. Mindful of her errand, she set herself to wander the room, taking a swift inventory of all the jewels on display. Lady Alicia's ample bosom was liberally decorated with a set of good diamonds, much too prominent to be stolen over the course of the evening. But was it wise of her to show them off them so? Perhaps she had not yet heard of the jewel-thief.

Several other ladies were similarly adorned: a Mrs. Bidden wore fine garnets in her ears; the throat of a Miss Hepworth was charmingly embraced by a necklace of fine pearls; and a tall, severe-looking fellow introduced as Mr. Tate had thrust a sapphire pin into the folds of his cravat.

All very promising, Gussie thought, and set herself to make notes: not only a catalogue of the tempting jewels she saw, but also the names of all the guests, for were anything to go missing after the revelry of this evening, she would find it useful to have a record of everyone who had been present to be tempted by them.

But no sooner had she formed the thought, and sought a quiet corner to retire into with her pocket-book and pencil, than another of the guests caught her eye. She had not immediately perceived him, for he had followed her own inclination, and tucked himself away in an alcove; but she plainly saw him now, and it was Lord Maundevyle.

He was not best pleased to see Gussie, it seemed, for having caught her eye his own was hastily withdrawn, and redirected towards the floor. He turned, seemingly desirous of entering into conversation with anybody to hand, as quickly as possible. Determined to avoid her, in other words, and Gussie smothered a small, most unwelcome stab of hurt.

There must be some explanation. He was most likely being absurd about the damage he had done to her uncle's roof, and if so, it was high time he stopped.

Accordingly, she marched over to him, with a smile as gracious (she hoped) as her aunt's was wont to be), and held out her hand to him. 'Lord Maundevyle, what a pleasure. We have become quite strangers to one another, have we not?'

He faced her with laudable courage, but she read in his eye the resignation of a man facing disaster with no hope of escape. He looked very well, she was bound to admit, his dark hair arranged with as much precision as Theo's, his attire still more fashionable. He did not smile as he bowed to her. 'Miss Werth. An unexpected pleasure, indeed.'

'Yes, it is odd of us to begin making appearances in society, is not it? A whim of my aunt's. She thought it advisable.' She might, once, have told him the real truth, and given him a share in the adventure. But not now, not when he was being so distant.

'Lady Alicia seems very well pleased,' Lord Maundevyle remarked.

Gussie's already thin patience expired. 'She does,' she replied, rather tartly, 'but you do not. Had you resolved upon avoiding us forever?'

His lordship appeared to be experiencing some difficulty in meeting her eye. 'I can hardly suppose my presence welcome,' he muttered.

'Come now, you cannot imagine it likely that we would hold a grudge against you? After all, it was only a little fire.'

'I am informed that fully half of the roof was burned away, with some damage also to the garrets.'

'Precisely,' Gussie agreed. 'Scarcely anything to speak of.'

This drew a smile, however small, and reluctant, from Lord Maundevyle. 'And what would you consider to be a house-fire worthy of note?'

'You forget that we are in London because of the fire at the Towers. A great many rooms were damaged, and the repairs are likely to continue for some months yet.'

'You have not been blessed with excellent fortune, I think, and I am sorry to have contributed to your run of ill luck.'

'In truth, I have been far more put out by your guilt than I was by your fire-breathing. Come, may we not be friends again?' Gussie fixed him with a challenging stare, in which, though she knew it not, there lay a small but perceptible degree of beseeching.

Lord Maundevyle perceived it, and began to look a little brighter. 'And your uncle? Does he agree?'

'Since the burden of managing the repairs all falls to him, he was, I believe, a little longer discomposed. But it is all forgotten now. See, here is my aunt to reassure you.'

Lady Werth was indeed approaching with every appearance of friendliness. 'Lord Maundevyle. Delightful.'

'Lady Werth,' said his lordship, bowing.

Her ladyship dropped her voice. 'I see Gussie has been drawing you into our clandestine fellowship. We shall be very glad of your assistance, to be sure.'

Lord Maundevyle looked, warily, from Lady Werth to Gussie. 'In fact, ma'am, she has been soundly chiding me for some one or two sins, and I believe she has not yet finished.'

'He has been so unfriendly, Aunt, I felt sure he could have no interest in our mission.'

'The best way to establish such a point, is to ask,' came the reply, far too reasonably.

'Besides which,' Gussie went on, 'I am not at all sure that he deserves to share another adventure. He did not seem especially well pleased with the last one.'

Lord Maundevyle hesitated. 'I hope it is not to end with mesmerism,' he ventured. 'Again. If it is, Miss Werth, then I fear you must excuse me.'

'A poor sort of adventure it would be, were I able to answer that question with any certainty,' Gussie retorted. 'It is the nature of daring endeavours to be unpredictable, I believe.'

Lady Werth intervened. 'Should you find yourself at a loss for an activity, Lord Maundevyle, and disposed to lend us your assistance, you will find my husband and son at cards.' With which decisive words, she laid a hand briefly upon Gussie's shoulder, and went away.

'You *were* awfully bored, were not you?' said Gussie, having recognised the signs.

'Dreadfully,' he agreed. 'But boredom may sometimes be considered preferable to various of the alternatives.'

'I shall think you very poor-spirited if you should bow out,' Gussie warned.

'You confuse me, Miss Werth. A moment ago you forbade me any part in this mysterious project, declaring me undeserving. Now I shall be undeserving if I do *not* participate.'

'Indeed, I often find myself in two minds about you,' Gussie answered. His querying look she ignored, not choosing to elaborate upon such a point. 'Well, the moment for decision has come. Are you to pitch in, or not?'

Lord Maundevyle eyed her sideways. He had lost his woe-begone look, to her satisfaction, and had regained those traces of wry amusement which had always rather enchanted her. 'I do not believe I ever had any choice,' he said, and left her side, heading, with a lively enough step, for the card-tables.

'Excellent,' murmured Gussie under her breath. She groped again for her pocket-book, and completed her lists; jewels in one column, attendees in another. Then, restoring the volume to her reticule – really, she was becoming very well satisfied to have such a volume always at hand; it was a wonder she had never thought to do so before – she re-entered the fray.

CHAPTER FIVE

22ND APRIL

*Gussie will never own herself disappointed, being disposed, al-
ways, to look ahead to the next exciting event (as she would term
them) rather than bemoaning the outcome of those that have concluded. Were she not of such a disposition, I believe she would declare herself most disappointed in Lady Alicia's execrable evening
party. As would I. A stultifying event in its every particular, and
not a single jewel missing by the end of it! The over-dressed tabbies
and tomcats took themselves off in the early hours of the morning,
as did we, and a waste of an evening it all was.*

*Mama, though, is undeterred. I need not add that Gussie has
suffered no check whatsoever to her enthusiasm, either.*

*Maundevyle was there. Had some conversation with him –
he has read the article in last week's Mayfair Gazette about
revenants, and had some few remarks to make upon it. Sensible
enough fellow, Maundevyle.*

*No sign of his sister and brother, not to mention Lady Maun-
devyle. Good. Father has enlisted Maundevyle's aid with Bal-*

lantine's absurd investigation, but I cannot say that we any of us achieved very much. I have the names of two gentlemen attendees who, gossip informs us, are said to be short of funds. Ballantine may have them, for all the good they may do.

I return forthwith to my reading, and trust I shall not be betrayed into such another evening again.

Theo's wish was not to be granted. His mother and Gussie he might have withstood, were they to approach him about any more dismal soirees. Even his father, he believed he would have roundly defied (*'Vingt-et-un! And whist! A thousand times, no!'*). But fate, it would seem, had a mind to intervene; and how could a mere Lord Bedgberry, however determined, resist the unstoppable tide of destiny?

'WHAT *IS* GOING ON?' he was later heard to remark, having tidied himself away into his father's book-room, and settled himself near the window, with a promising pile of volumes at his elbow. A mere half-hour's peaceful study had he enjoyed before the tumult interrupted him; feet rapidly passing back and forth outside the door, to be specific, and more distant doors banging, and a chatter of voices somewhere in the house.

Having stuck his tousled head out into the corridor (Daundelyon had yet to break him of his habit of tugging at his rust-coloured locks, when distressed, or merely deep in thought) he had witnessed Gussie sailing past, clearly in high gig. Close on her heels floated Great-Aunt Honoria's head, babbling away about something or other.

'Oh! Theo!' said his great-aunt, pausing before him. In her excitement, a few droplets of blood leaked from her severed neck, and spattered over the tiled floor. 'The shockingest thing!'

'*Most* shocking, not "shockingest",' Theo corrected automatically.

A single, severed hand appeared and waved this off. 'Never mind that! Do come and see.' She drifted off after Gussie, rippling with laughter.

Theo, correctly surmising that he was not to have a moment's peace for some time, heaved a sigh, and exited the book-room. He trailed down the passage after his cousin and aunt, and found them gathered in the front hall – together with his father, his mother, Great-Uncle Silvester, Goodspeed, and Clarissa Selwyn. Two of the housemaids lingered at the door of the parlour, paused in their daily efforts at cleaning it, he supposed; and one of the footmen stood at the front door, which stood open.

Someone had arrived, he surmised. A person of the utmost *shockingest*, clearly.

'What is going on?' he said again, pushing past Gussie.

The doorway was empty; no one stood there. He glanced about, but saw no sign of a guest, besides Clarissa Selwyn. Was it *she* who had somehow created this ruckus? He would not have put it past her.

'It is an invitation!' declared Great-Aunt Honoria. 'An invitation of the very best sort! Highly exclusive. Everything of the *most* select.'

'Another party,' sighed Theo, unable to see why the prospect of such should have brought the whole house to the door.

Gussie intercepted him as he attempted to flee. 'Look, Theo,' she ordered, pointing out into the street.

A cloudy April morning waited out there, free of rain and sun alike. 'I don't see—' he began, and stopped, for suddenly, he *did* see.

A carriage had drawn up in the street, an equipage which had not, at first, excited Theo's particular notice. Several other townhouses flanked that of the Werth family, and most of their occupants possessed their own carriage-and-four; vehicles and well-matched horses were often to be seen taking up handsomely-dressed ladies, or setting down gentlemen returned from their clubs.

This one was different. It bore no distinguishing arms upon its glossily black-painted doors, nor any other distinctive characteristic. The style, Theo dimly recognised, was modern: a travelling chariot, enclosing its occupants behind walls and dim windows, with a team of four black horses to pull it.

It was the absence of the coachman that finally penetrated his befuddlement, though that was not so very strange. Why did his imagination immediately leap to the conclusion that there had never been a coachman? That the vehicle, by some means, drove itself? The fellow had in all probability stepped down for a moment, or had yet to mount the box.

But that could not explain away its strangeness, for it looked rather as though the shining wheels were hovering some few inches off the ground.

Indeed, so were the lacquered hooves of the horses.

Before Theo had time to absorb these startling facts, let alone to comment upon them, the carriage's door opened and somebody stepped out. A footman, of sorts, for the fellow's black-and-silver attire had the crisp, regimental neatness of livery. But footmen did not usually ride inside chariots like gentlemen, and this one moved with the confidence and poise of the Quality.

The bow he made to the assembled Werths was all politeness, but lacking entirely in the deference typical of a servant.

He did not speak, merely handed a letter to Lady Werth. A handsome thing in itself, that, creamy parchment sealed with royal purple wax.

'There it is!' exulted Great-Aunt Honoria. 'What did I tell you!'

Theo's attention strayed from the letter, even as his mother broke the seal and unfolded it. Something about the footman struck him as peculiar, and at length he realised what it was.

Beneath the silvery wig, and masculine attire notwithstanding, this footman was no man at all, but a woman. Her face, smooth and oval and of indeterminate age, remained impassive as she awaited Lady Werth's response, but her eye briefly caught Theo's, and twinkled.

Gussie, leaning over her aunt's arm to catch a glimpse of the letter, read aloud: 'The Grand Masquerade Ball for the Wyrde and Wondrous.' She gave a little, incredulous laugh. 'How grand it sounds! I can only imagine it is a jest of some sort.'

'It is no jest, my dear!' said Great-Aunt Honoria, bobbing with excitement.

'But I have never heard of such a thing in all of my life. Aunt? Uncle? Have you?'

Lord Werth shook his head; his wife was too much absorbed by the invitation to reply. But Great-Aunt Honoria would have none of it. 'That is only because it has not been held in so very long a time! It was quite the thing in my youth, I assure you. Not that it was any regular occurrence. No, it was held only once every thirteen years, either at Beltane or All Hallow's Eve. The grandest event of any season! Many a person would have *killed* for an invitation.'

'We have had ours,' put in Clarissa, her attention almost as occupied by the footwoman as Theo's. 'Not an hour ago, and I came here at *once* to see if you had got one, too.'

'Lord Maundevyle accepted, I suppose?' said Gussie dubiously.

'Henry! Of course he did. If he had not, I do believe Mamma would have slaughtered him where he stood.' She lowered her voice, leaned a little nearer Gussie, and added, indicating the bearer of the invitation, 'I do believe I would look well in just such an ensemble. Would not I?'

Lady Werth, at last, looked up from the letter. 'You await a response?' she asked of the footwoman.

The woman inclined her head.

'Well?' said Lady Werth, raising her voice: clearly an enquiry of her family.

'Oh, *do* let's,' said Gussie.

'No!' exclaimed Theo in horror.

'Without a doubt!' carolled Great-Aunt Honoria.

'You must come!' said Clarissa. 'It will scarcely be any fun at all if you do not.'

Lady Werth looked at her husband. Theo was, briefly, heartened to note that his father's face was impenetrably grave; he would forbid it, of course, and there would be an end to the business.

'We are not to know, I suppose, who our hosts are to be?' asked Lord Werth.

Lady Werth handed him the letter, and a brief perusal seemingly answered his lordship's question.

He gave a small sigh, and said: 'I am wearied of mysteries, I confess, but this one intrigues me against my will.'

'Then we go!' cried Great-Aunt Honoria.

'We do indeed.' Lord Werth bowed to the footwoman, who bowed back, and straightened. 'You will be called for in one week,' she announced, and withdrew into the strange carriage once more. The door closed upon her, and the vehicle drove away, or rather, floated; the wheels made no pretence of turning.

'I have not looked forward to *anything* so much in an *age*,' declared Honoria, and drifted off, presumably to regale Ivo Farthing with the impending delights.

'One week,' Gussie mused. 'Did not my aunt mention Beltane? In a week it will only be the twenty-ninth.'

'It is to be held over several days, I believe,' said Lady Werth, and handed the letter to her niece. 'See there, it says: the masquerade ball is to be the closing event, not the only event.'

'*Days* of mysterious revelry!' crowed Clarissa. 'And did you mark the carriage? It flies! I declare! I never saw such a thing.'

Theo, his wishes and dreads unattended to, slunk away. He had no illusions about being suffered to decline the invitation, and shut himself up in the book-room. The invitation had been made to *all* the Werths, and all the Werths must endure it alike.

No one could prevent him from taking some part of the library along with him, however. He might contrive to spend the chief part of the events in his own room, *alone*, and dancing be damned.

CHAPTER SIX

I need hardly state the extent of my excitement. A masquerade ball! Hosted by a mysterious and unnamed person! In a location we are not to know until the moment of arrival! Could anything be more perfectly peculiar?

Poor Theo looked ready to kill us all before consenting to join our party, but that is only his way. Some few days have passed since the invitation arrived and not one of us has departed this mortal coil, so I endeavour to hope that my disreputable cousin will bear the torment somehow.

My aunt says that Mr. Ballantine is to join us, and I confess myself pleased. He is as much a Werth as the rest of us, after all – if only by some convoluted connection – and the affair would seem sadly flat without all of us there. Quite apart from which, what better opportunity for a jewel-thief than a series of glittering balls, at which every Wyrded person of rank, station and wealth is sure to be present? There will be a great deal to investigate, even as we enjoy ourselves.

That reminds me: I am informed I must better organise my notes. Mr. Ballantine insists upon it. He took my offerings from last week's parties and frowned awfully over them.

'A gentleman in a green coat,' he read aloud, scowling at my guest list as though it had offered him some intolerable insult. 'Moss-green rather than forest green; reddish hair, and a slight limp.' Then he looked at me with those scowling brows and said, 'What am I to make of this, Miss Werth?'

'I never did hear his name,' I explained. 'Or perhaps I did, and forgot it again, and my aunt did not remember it either.'

'A thin lady in an unflattering shade of yellow,' he read next. 'Nose like a fish-hook.'

And then he stared at me so thunderously I might have proceeded so far as to quail, were I capable of such flutterings.

I smiled instead. 'I am sure it is a very good description,' I said firmly. 'And you may soon find out to whom it pertains, with a very little effort.'

He sighed, and put my page of notes away into his own pocket-book. 'I suppose I might, at that,' he allowed. 'But I should be much obliged if you would engage in these "little efforts" yourself, Miss Werth, and furnish me with proper names.'

I must own that he is right – privately, at least. Nothing could have persuaded me to acknowledge him correct to his face.

First, though, I shall employ my little efforts in pursuit of another mystery, for the masquerade ball is almost upon us. We depart tomorrow! And so distracted have I been with Mr. Ballantine's errands, I have yet to fully investigate the pressing question of the ball. Just who is responsible for this enigmatic revelry, and why should they insist upon such secrecy?

I shall begin with a full interrogation of Great-Aunt Honoria, if she can be persuaded to speak plainly. She is the only one of us who seems to have any prior knowledge of the event, after all.

'Oh!' said that lady, soon afterwards. 'But it is very well known, indeed! I cannot *think* how it comes about that none of you should ever have heard of the Grand Masquerade.'

Gussie had set down her pen, closed up her journal, and set off for the attic rooms directly, and had found her ghostly great-aunt in a huddle with Ivo Farthing, as usual. They had adopted the most decrepit of the attic garrets for their own hideaway, for reasons best known to themselves; Gussie thought it wisest not to enquire.

Amid the drifting cobwebs and choking dust, Great-Aunt Honoria floated like a smiling nightmare, her powdered white hair piled high upon her head, and adorned with delicate bones. The head of Ivo Farthing was never far distant from his fair beloved; round-cheeked and smiling, he, the neatly severed line of his neck concealed beneath the shrouding folds of an ivory cravat. He beamed upon Gussie as she knocked and entered, a figure of jocularity and bonhomie.

'Well, but nobody has,' Gussie said in answer to her aunt. 'Is that not strange? But you said, Aunt, that the Ball was a regular occurrence in your youth. I hope you will forgive my pointing out that your youth was many years ago.'

Great-Aunt Honoria pondered this. 'Perhaps it was,' she allowed. 'When you are as old as me, my dear, you will soon give up counting the passage of time. It is enough to send a lady into a decline.'

'Ah! But the years haven't touched you at all,' interposed Mr. Farthing, wreathed in smiles. 'You remain as beautiful as a snowdrop, my dear.'

Great-Aunt Honoria developed a rosy blush, a manoeuvre Gussie beheld with some interest. How her long-dead revenant of an Aunt could contrive to blush was its own little mystery; one which, in all likelihood, she would never understand. The effect, however, was charming.

'Oh, Ivo,' simpered Honoria. 'You flatter me.'

'Well, but,' Gussie interjected, before they could carry themselves away in sentiment. 'What I mean to ask, is: if the Ball was held every thirteen years some hundred years ago, and never since, what should suddenly revive it now? Do you not recall anything about it that might be pertinent, Aunt?'

'Nothing at all,' came the airy answer. 'One did not ask such questions, you understand. One was far too busy *enjoying* oneself.' Her floating head began a waltzing, bobbing dance about the garret as she hummed a dreamy tune. 'Dancing every night! Games and revelries! Banquets of the very best provender! You shall soon see, my dear. Oh, *how* I have missed it.'

'I only wish for one clue,' Gussie persisted. 'Just one, Aunt. Surely you remember some little thing that I may investigate?'

Great-Aunt Honoria did not seem to hear. She was humming again, louder this time, and Ivo Farthing was joining her in her macabre dance.

'Oh, very well,' Gussie sighed, and turned to go.

'The carriage!' said her great-aunt abruptly. 'Not the same equipage, I perceived. A new one entirely, I should think. In my day, it was a grand coach, fit for a king and queen. And so it is today, only altered.'

'Rather dark and unremarkable for royalty,' Gussie disagreed. 'Save for the fact that it flies.'

'Ah yes; it flies.' Great-Aunt Honoria whirled past in a haze of icy mist, wreathed like streamers through her hair. 'That, at least, has not changed.'

'Is there anything else you can remember, Aunt?' Gussie pleaded.

'It was always held in the same house,' came the answer. 'I attended twice, in my time, and though I never had the smallest idea *where* the place was, it was certainly the *same*. A palace, rather! Quite the grandest abode I ever beheld. And the servants all wore the black-and-silver livery – *so* discreet, every one of them. And our hosts dressed in those colours, too; the Lord and the Lady, we called them, and never any other name did we know. *She* so very beautiful, and *he* everything that is handsome! Though never were they seen without a striking domino apiece.'

This was far better; Gussie retrieved a pencil and her journal, and hastily wrote down every word uttered by her aunt. 'Well, go on,' she prompted when her aunt fell silent.

'That is all!' carolled the revenant. 'The rest is only a blur of dancing and dining and intrigue. I cannot remember a *thing* more.' The giggle which accompanied this statement aroused Gussie's suspicions of it not being entirely truthful, but she had done questioning her aunt. There would be no getting anything more out of Honoria while she was engaged in the waltz; she was doing it again now, Ivo partnering her, their two heads weaving serenely around one another.

Gussie thanked them politely, though her words were, in all likelihood, unheard. She went away to peruse her gleanings in private, absorbed in thought. Honoria had given her no obvious direction for her enquiries, but she had learned a great deal regardless. A picture of the revelries to come was forming in her mind, and the vision, being made up of equal parts vibrant life and sinister mystery, pleased and intrigued her very much indeed.

The chief question turning through her thoughts pertained to the host and hostess. The Lord, and the Lady! How enigmatic, and how intriguing. Who were the mysterious pair, and what should prompt them to conceal their identities so?

More importantly still: a hundred years had passed. Were the same lady and gentleman behind the revival of the ball? Or was this somebody else's party?

Gussie's curiosity would not, could not, be suppressed. Come what may, she resolved to find out.

APRIL 28TH

I have been cloistered at the townhouse these several days, compelled to remain by my father's deep frowns and my mother's frigid silences alike. They suspect me of a plot to escape the ball, of course, and they are perfectly right: if I thought I could get away with a demurral, I would decline at once, and disappear to my rooms forthwith.

But I would never hear the end of it. And, like it or not, amends must yet be made for the devastation of the Towers, though it was not my fault of course. If suffering through a dance or two will do the trick, I'll endure it somehow.

Great-Uncle Silvester found his way back to the family abode eventually. I saw him yesterday, flitting about the kitchens and scaring Cook half to death. I did not choose to interrupt so blameless a pastime, for I am sure he was enjoying himself immensely.

He came flapping after me, however, as I withdrew to the book-room, and settled atop the tall back of one of the library-chairs, tearing the wood to shreds with his stone claws.

Just as I was taking up a book, he spoke.

'Taking a turn about the gardens, eh? Most refreshing.'

'No, Uncle,' I replied. 'As you can plainly see, I am engaged in study.' I accompanied these words with a pointed glare – why must people turn sociable just when a man takes up a book?

Great-Uncle Silvester nodded and chuckled and shuffled about and I thought, for a moment, that he would consent to be quiet.

But no.

'May I,' he said abruptly, 'claim the first two dances, Miss Wetherby?'

'Well, of course you may come to the ball with us, Uncle,' I answered, without looking up. 'Indeed, I believe Mother will insist.'

This pleased the old man, for some reason; he gave his horrible, grinding chuckle and flapped his stone grotesque's wings. 'Meet me in the library,' he whispered, and laughed. 'Not before midnight, mind! And not after!'

'The library,' I said aloud, much struck. 'Why, of course! It is a house party, is not it? Several days of nonsense to be got through? Surely there will be a book-room somewhere about the place.' I cheered at once. Perhaps there would be titles of great antiquity to be perused; I might even make some interesting discovery. 'Thank you, Uncle,' I said. 'I am very much obliged to you for the thought.'

He launched himself from the back of the chair and took up a crazed flight around the book-room, flapping stone dust into my eyes with each swooping circuit. He was gabbling something, but there was no making out what it might be, and I wasn't much interested.

'Steady on, old man,' I protested, shaking out the pages of my book. 'Quiet, if you will. I've a great deal to get through before tomorrow.'

He fell into a paroxysm of coughing and vanished through the door. I heard him coughing still, all the way down the corridor and away to who-knows-where, and then, finally, peace reigned once again.

I was able to finish Ashton's "Preservation of Corpses" after that, and a good thing, too. Who knows but what Great-Aunt Honoria may require some maintenance, if she is to dance the night away three or four nights together.

Theo expected Daundelyon to make a great bother of himself, hassling his master about proper garments for various occasions, and the packing of a portmanteau, and whatnot besides. In fact, the valet scarcely troubled Theo at all; once his lordship had been successfully inserted into his trousers, waistcoat and blue cutaway, Theo saw nothing more of him until the time came to undress him for bed.

'I suppose I'll be wanting all manner of fine articles for the balls,' he grumbled as the tight-fitting coat was carefully winched from his shoulders.

'I daresay, milord,' agreed Daundelyon.

Theo racked his brains. 'Um. Breeches and buckles and all that, isn't it? No?'

'Perhaps, milord,' said Daundelyon. 'I understand the Grand Masquerade to be an old tradition come back again, and cannot suppose the fashions should be very current. But I've packed trousers for you as well.'

'You have? And shoes and waistcoats and cravats, and everything?'

'Yes, milord. And your shaving gear. Boots and coats in case there should be any riding to be had. Two great-coats and three

of your best waistcoats. All the shirts a body could want, and
twenty fresh cravats. Breeches and stockings and coats: the other
blue, the dark green and the new claret your mother ordered. A
diamond pin that was your grandfather's, so Milord Werth told
me, that's to go in your neck-cloth. Mourning bands and black
coat and cravats—'

'Hold on.' Theo had heard most of this with mounting incredulity, even as Daundelyon busied himself removing Theo's
boots and carefully restoring his discarded garments to the clos-
et. 'Mourning clothes? What?'

'Yes, milord.' Daundelyon nodded his head emphatically as
he brushed dust from Theo's dark blue cutaway. 'Never know
when you might need to show some respect.'

'For the freshly deceased?'

'Aye, sir.'

Daundelyon did not, it seemed, see fit to elaborate, but after
a moment's reflection Theo supposed he hardly needed to. A
house full of the wealthy and Wyrded for days together, several
of them Selwyns or Werths? The wonder would rather be for
everyone to make it out alive.

'I suppose you're right,' Theo muttered, thinking longingly
of books and libraries and an absence of people, living or dead.
'I'm glad you thought of it,' he added, aware that his attitude
thus far had been one of unrelieved surliness towards his new
valet and abruptly regretting the fact. Goodness, what if his
father were to pop off in the midst of the waltz? Or Gussie? And

he without a single black coat in his portmanteau! He would be hearing about it forever.

'My pleasure, milord,' said Daundelyon, and withdrew.

THE MORROW FOUND THE noble Werth household in a state of unusual harmony – or, at least, of common purpose and preparation. Theo had not, as yet, recovered what passed for his temper, but as a silent and brooding demeanour was in no way out of character for him – whether it was the product of ill-humour or mere abstraction of thought – nobody paid him any heed.

Gussie had acquired several new gowns, on purpose for the revelries. Theo only knew this because she had mentioned it – repeatedly. And now, he supposed without much interest, she was wearing one of them: an airy confection of a thing in some purplish colour, with which she appeared highly pleased, for she would not refrain from swishing the skirts about whenever she turned.

Theo had been squeezed into an ensemble Daundelyon assured him was "very much the thing": the claret-coloured coat, and articles of like character. He stood stiffly ill-at-ease in this unaccustomed finery as the disparate scions of his disreputable family milled about him in a fever of activity: Gussie twirling up and down the passages and posing in the doorways; his mother and father both in a state of mental abstraction, occasionally

glimpsed passing by at some short distance; Miss Frostell packing sundry articles into Gussie's portmanteau, none appearing
to be of any great use; Great-Aunt Honoria and Great-Uncle
Silvester swooping about the ceilings, chattering and laughing
in a fashion fit to break Theo's head.

When Mr. Ballantine finally arrived, Theo found himself
with a companion in uneasy silence. The Runner joined him
in the hall, where Theo had tidied himself somewhat out of the
way; the two exchanged only brief syllables.

'All ready, are we?' said Mr. Ballantine, softly.

'No,' Theo replied, casting a weary eye over the twin visions
of Lady Werth, sailing from the great stairs in the direction of
the kitchens; and Miss Frostell, traipsing from the best parlour
towards the cloak-room, with what urgent mission of mercy in
mind he could not have said.

Mr. Ballantine nodded. 'Can't be long now.'

'No,' Theo said again, for the day was wearing away, and the
sun lowering in the sky. There had been questions raised as to
exactly when on the 28th the dark carriage ought to be expected
to return; Great-Aunt Honoria had put paid to all speculation by saying, firmly and with all the smug certainty of prior
experience, 'Oh! After nightfall, to be sure. Nothing happens
until midnight, at the Masquerade.' And she had laughed in a
strange way, which Theo might have found to be foreboding of
something, if he had troubled himself to care.

Theo roused himself enough to say, with a decent appearance
of mild interest: 'Catch your thief yet?'

'No,' answered Mr. Ballantine, which was, it seemed, all that was to be said on the subject, for he fell silent again.

The two men waited in mutual suspense and, perhaps, mutual solidarity as their myriad relations completed their toilets; made last-minute (but vital) alterations to their packing arrangements; and bustled about the house setting purposeless things in order for the several days of their collective absence. These trifling errands at last completed, they drifted, one by one, into the hall, forming, over a long half-hour, a large and lavish group of wealthy, Wyrded Werths in a state of high suspense.

It seemed an age before the knocker sounded. Goodspeed leapt to open the door: and there, waiting, was the footwoman who had delivered the invitation, a week before. If Theo entertained any doubt that it might be the same person, he was encouraged to greater certainty when she caught his eye, and – did he mistake it? – winked.

'Lords and Ladies,' she said with a low bow, the silver gilt on her tricorner hat glinting in the moonlight. 'Your carriage.'

The same dark, beautiful equipage lurked at the kerb, gently afloat, and lit with silver lamps. Theo looked in vain for a second such vehicle, and preferably a third; only one waited there. 'Will we all *fit*, though?' he muttered.

He was not heard, or at least, he was not attended to. Lord and Lady Werth stepped forward directly, as the footmen prepared to load their luggage. Gussie, of course, was in immediate pursuit, and Great-Aunt Honoria with Ivo. The four disappeared into the carriage without visible difficulty; Great-Uncle Silvester followed.

Goodspeed, Daundelyon, Hayton and Mr. Ballantine were all, he realised, waiting for him.

'There isn't room,' he protested.

A window was let down inside the carriage, and Gussie's face appeared. 'Do hurry up, Theo!' she called.

Theo gave a sigh, and strode forward. If his absurd family required a lesson in capacity, well then, he would just have to oblige—

This amiable thought deserted him as soon as he reached the carriage, for he could plainly see that there remained plenty of room within.

'How...?' he began, but soon abandoned the subject; if the thing could float, why could it not also contort itself into un-usual capaciousness? He stepped in, and settled himself; soon afterwards came Mr. Ballantine, and Goodspeed and Daunde-lyon and, at last, Hayton.

The footwoman closed the doors upon them all, and dis-appeared somewhere. Theo waited, tense and uneasy, for the moment of departure. A lurking dread assailed him. Was the carriage going to roll along the street, like an ordinary equipage (or at least, only slightly above it?). Or was it going to—oh dear, there came a juddering, as the horses moved off, and then a *lurch*, moderately sickening; and an unmistakeable *swooping* feeling—they were airborne, they were absolutely airborne, and Theo's stomach pitched into his mouth.

'I do not—like—*flying*,' he was able to utter, in a choked and futile protest, clinging to his seat with a white-knuckled grip.

'It will soon be over,' murmured his mother, soothingly.

'In all likelihood we will be in motion some time,' Gussie disagreed. 'But you need not look out of the window, Theo, if you do not like it.'

He did *not* like it, not one bit; but his unaccountable cousin did, for she hung over the window herself, her face blocking it entirely, a light of strange glee in her shining eyes.

Theo closed his with a groan, and sat back to suffer.

CHAPTER SEVEN

GUSSIE'S FIRST THOUGHT REGARDING the mysterious manor of the enigmatic masquerade was that it gave a good impression of total abandonment.

The reason for the coach's not only floating but flying soon became clear: the house was not in London. Indeed, it may not even have been situated in England. The carriage soared very high before, at last, it swooped down to land; Gussie, watching avidly out of the window, witnessed the distant glimmer of early stars winking to life in a darkening sky, soon obscured by eerie drifts of chill white mist. They plunged earthwards at such a speed, Gussie felt certain, for one exhilarating instant, that they must surely be dashed to pieces against the ground. Theo (overtaken by terror, poor soul) uttered a strangled shriek, and fell against Gussie's shoulder.

But the landing came gently enough, and they were set down in the midst of a high, craggy space ringed by jagged peaks.

The house not being immediately visible, Gussie turned her attention to the snow-dusted valley instead, and found it acceptable. As the footwoman opened the door and set down a step, Gussie welcomed the biting chill of the evening air, the light dusting of snowflakes upon her upturned face, and the general air of isolation into which she emerged.

'Yes,' she murmured to the empty air, smiling. 'One expects to be set upon any moment, by wolves perhaps, or crazed ruffians. Though one must not be too particular: really, any manner of violence at all would be a treat.'

'Do not say so, my dear,' said Miss Frostell with a shudder, tiptoeing towards her erstwhile charge as though she might contrive to float above the snow like the carriage, if only she were to step lightly enough. 'I am sure we shall be safe, what with these sturdy footmen about us.'

'Footpersons, Frosty,' answered Gussie bracingly. 'They are not all men, as I am sure you will have observed.'

'Very true, and curious it is.'

'For my part I consider it perfectly natural. Why should not women wear trousers, and carry pistols?'

Mr. Ballantine answered her. 'I ought to have known you would take such a view of it, Miss Werth.'

'Indeed you ought, and I am by no means in despair of carrying my point with you at last.'

'You should not like to become a footwoman instead, I suppose?'

'Instead of a Runner? No indeed. Though,' she added, struck by a fresh thought, 'Perhaps a highwaywoman might suit me just as well, if not better. What do you think, Mr. Ballantine? Upon which side of the law shall I cast my future?'

'That is blackmail,' he observed. 'And quite useless. You forget I have no right of interest in your future whatsoever.'

'So if it should please me to become a criminal, I am full welcome to do so as far as you are concerned.'

'Yes. Though I shall be bound to catch you at it sooner or later, and I shall be very severe upon you when I do.'

'How attractive a prospect,' Gussie murmured.

Mr. Ballantine studied her face. 'I cannot tell whether or not that remark is sincere.'

'Oh, she is only funning, Mr. Ballantine,' interjected Miss Frostell.

'Naturally,' said Gussie, smiling her blandest smile.

Mr. Ballantine only eyed her narrowly, and gave up the point, proving himself a man of sense.

Everyone being by now alighted from the carriage, and clustered together in the midst of a growing storm of snow, Gussie began to imagine that something must soon occur. Nothing did, for a time; the footwomen closed up the carriage and the coachman drove away, taking all their luggage with them, and silence fell.

The cold deepened.

'I see we have been abandoned here to die,' Gussie observed into the hush. 'A clever plan. Neither wolves nor ruffians after all, merely a slow expiration from exposure and deprivation.'

'But how delightful,' Great-Aunt Honoria enthused, her cheerful tones drifting down from somewhere high above.

Gussie tilted up her chin, but could not see her aunt through the thickening mist. 'Is it the prospect of our imminent demise that so delights you, Aunt, or have you seen something?'

She was not answered, but no response was necessary, for abruptly the mist began to clear; streamed away upon twin gusts of wind, like a curtain parting.

And out of the darkening night loomed the forbidding shape of a grand mansion – nay, a palace, for in size and grandeur it merited no lesser name. The hulking structure swallowed up the sky, vast and impenetrable, its façade a map of dark, gaping windows, twisting pilasters and chimneys, and carved grotesques crouched atop mouldings and frames like lurking nightmares. Gussie was enchanted.

As the Werths watched, spellbound, pale ghost-lights flared to life in every window. More such glimmering wisps illuminated a long, wide set of stairs sweeping down from the vast double doors to the valley below.

A whisper broke the silence. *'Welcome,'* it uttered, in a deep, shattering susurration scarcely human.

Slowly, the silver-gilded doors swung open.

Great-Aunt Honoria gave a whoop of joy. She and Ivo Farthing were the first to ascend the stairs, their smiling heads
bobbing and swooping up and up towards the palace.

Gussie exchanged a look with Theo. He appeared pale, perhaps from the journey, and apprehensive, perhaps from a life-
long want of spirit.

'You first, cousin,' she offered.

He responded with a sardonic smile. 'We are in polite society
now, are not we? The rules of precedence must be observed.'
And, with an exaggerated sweep of his arm, he bowed to his
mother and father.

'So they must,' agreed Lady Werth.

'Shall we?' said her husband, offering her his arm.

Lady Werth took it with a tight little smile, and the Werths set
forth, Lord Bedgberry and Gussie falling in behind the leaders
of their house, and Mr. Ballantine, Miss Frostell, Goodspeed,
Daundelyon, and Hayton bringing up the rear.

Great-Uncle Silvester was nowhere in evidence, which delighted Gussie, for it could only mean he had gone ahead already. What might not he discover, flitting from window to
window in his dark shadow of a shape, perfectly at home and
unremarkable above a hundred other grotesques?

'Whatever mysteries this house holds,' she announced, 'I am
determined to find them all out. Every single one.'

'Far be it from me to dampen your spirits, cousin,' Theo
muttered, 'but you ought, perhaps, be careful what you wish
for.'

'I have considered being careful,' answered Gussie. 'Tried it, even, on some long-ago day. I scarcely remember it now, for it was not entertaining at all.'

APRIL 29TH

I write from the hushed sanctity of our chambers inside the Palace of Nightmares (as I confidently expect it to prove). My aunt, being wearied from the journey, retired immediately to bed, but the hour is not yet so far advanced, barely past ten o'clock; for my own part, I am too intrigued to sleep.

Frosty, I feel, has not taken so well to our environs. As we advanced up those imposing stairs, we found nobody awaiting us; no sign of the Lord and Lady Great-Aunt Honoria spoke of. Only that distant voice, so strange, which uttered not another word save that "Welcome", and the rest has been silence.

Even the servants hardly spoke. They are all dressed alike, in black and silver livery, indistinct as to gender, and all enigmatic as the moon. Poor Frosty walked very close to me, bristling with unease, though nothing has yet occurred to warrant such caution. She is now installed in a comfortable arm-chair, with a cup of hot tea and a plate of cake a footman was so obliging as to bring up from the kitchens. I trust she will soon be easy.

There is to be no revelry until the morrow, it appears; this evening is given over to the welcoming of myriad guests. We have what seems to be an entire wing of the house to ourselves, though I

am sure it is no such thing. Many bedchambers, including sepa-
rate ones for Goodspeed, Daundelyon and Hayton; two parlours,
a handsome one for the family and a comfortable one for our
servants; several dressing-rooms, bathing rooms, and sundry such
amenities; and even, to my uncle's delight (and Theo's), a small
book-room, with a reasonable selection of volumes. We could be
comfortable here for a month, in short, and I begin to wonder
(with a delicious frisson of terror) whether we are ever to be per-
mitted to leave.

For despite all these comforts, and a civil and attentive welcome,
there is a palpable air of anticipation; something faintly ominous,
even sinister. Perhaps my wishes lead me astray, and I imagine
this menace entirely. But Frosty's reaction suggests that it is no
invention of my own. She is not usually faint of heart.

Theo and my uncle have vanished into the book-room;
Great-Aunt Honoria and Ivo Farthing into some devilry else-
where in the house; Goodspeed and the others (including, I believe,
Mr. Ballantine) into their own sitting-room; and Frosty into the
depths of her beverage, leaving me alone with my journal.

I believe I shall explore the house.

If this should prove to be my last entry in this little book, know
that something terrible must have happened to me, on account of
which I have died a very happy woman.

So vast and shrouded in silence was the house, Gussie enjoyed
the pleasing sensation of total isolation as she set forth from her
own quarters and ventured into the corridors beyond.

This enjoyable experience persisted for some little time. The house might have been an abandoned half-ruin, for she met no one as she ventured along a winding passage, its walls covered in portraits of long-ago men and women. Up a handsome oak staircase wandered she, the gleaming wood untouched by dust, despite the spellbinding hush in the air; down again and down farther, into a little, echoing hall, a stormy mural of the tumultuous heavens splayed across its ceiling.

When at last the hush was broken, the babble of unfamiliar voices lashed the silence like a thundercrack, jarring to Gussie's ears.

Into the vaulted hall streamed a gaggle of ladies, all talking at once. Abruptly came Gussie to recall that the splendours of the house were no private entertainment for her family alone, but thrown open to other families as well. A great many other families.

'—did say that she will not travel without her own sheets, but to be sure, so fine a house must be well provided with—'

'Oh! Look at those cherubs! How *darling* – look, Fanny, do you see? The ceiling! If you will just tip your head back a very little – I do not believe your bonnet would fall—'

'—are those cherubs? I see but half a cherub, Antonia — scarcely more than a face – the other half having, I suppose, vanished into the maw of that delightful dragon—'

'—resembles Uncle Ned more than a little; was not he black-scaled? A wyvern, of course, not a dragon entire, but *uncanny*—'

'—always despised cherubs, indeed I do not know who does not—'

'—what *has* become of my reticule? It was safe in the carriage, here upon my left wrist, and now I do not know what I am to do, for it carried my spectacles—'

The ladies, five of them at least, did not immediately perceive Gussie, loitering as she was in the shadows. They were obliged to note her neat figure at last when two of them collided with it at once, and recoiled in a flurry of exclamation and apology.

'—something is there! I cannot determine – a spirit, perhaps?'

'—rather solid for a spirit, I should say, but my *spectacles*—'

'Good evening,' said Gussie, and if, in a spirit of mischief, she pitched her voice low, and cultivated a sinister tone, who could blame her?

'Oh!' declared two ladies at once, and, by some long-practiced instinct, dropped into curtseys. 'Forgive me, ma'am, for I did not see you there,' said one.

'It is another guest, dear, that is all,' said the other.

'Oh,' answered the first, disappointed.

Gussie perfectly understood. 'There will be spirits aplenty, later,' she offered. 'My own Great-Aunt Honoria is somewhere about the place, pleasingly devoid of life and limb, and I can only suppose there are more.'

The ladies brightened. 'We were to bring our cousin Walter with us,' said one. 'Only he was indisposed at the last moment—'

'How can a spirit be indisposed?' objected a third lady, coming forward. 'He has not been ill since he was alive, and he has not been *that* since Queen Anne's time. He did not want to come, depend upon it, but would not say so. How do you do, ma'am? May we introduce ourselves?' This lady had a breathless, hurried mode of speech, and was quite young, younger than her companions. She appeared fragile, thin and wispy, with light hair, though she moved with the same restless energy with which she spoke. 'I am Miss Jendring. My sisters Miss Cecily and Miss Fanny Jendring. My mother Mrs Jendring, and my aunt Mrs Whyting.'

'Miss Werth,' Gussie answered, making her curtsey. The Jendrings had brought no menfolk with them at all, it appeared; five women, all light-haired and neatly dressed, and as energetic as Miss Jendring herself. Their attire indicated they were of respectable, but not high status, with no titles amongst them, and no pretensions towards finery. Gussie liked them on sight.

'Werth!' uttered Mrs Jendring, in a booming way. 'That is a name we all know.' Her tone hinted at tales of misdemeanour and scandal.

'Thank you,' said Gussie, modestly.

'Do say we shall be friends,' put in Miss Cecily Jendring. 'I long to hear all about your cousin, Lord Bedgberry – is he as despicable as they say?'

'And your father,' added Miss Fanny. 'A corpse-raiser! How shocking! We only *wish* we had such a one among our family, but we are all rather ordinary in the Wyrded way, I'm afraid—'

'Hush, Fanny, how can you be so absurd?' said Mrs Whyting. 'There can be nothing *ordinary* about the Wyrde—'

Gussie, perceiving she would have to strive to be heard amongst the Jendrings, interjected. 'Lord Werth is my uncle. My parents are long dead, though my sister informs me they are both very well.'

'Your sister talks to the dead, does she?' said Mrs Whyting, nodding wisely. 'A sound Wyrde. Goodness, how well-supplied you all are!'

It being considered impolite to enquire directly as to the nature of another person's Wyrde, nobody asked that question of Gussie. But that it was implied was clear enough, for the Jendrings, remarkably, all stopped talking at once, and turned matching expressions of enquiry upon Gussie.

Gussie found herself uninterested in satisfying their curiosity. 'Lord Bedgberry is every bit as despicable as rumour suggests,' she said, choosing instead to answer Miss Cecily. 'He spends fully half his time locked away somewhere with a book, and would never venture out at all were he not sometimes compelled to do so. Only imagine how dull.'

Miss Cecily's eyes grew wide. She was very young, Gussie perceived – perhaps only eighteen – and had not yet outgrown her share of silliness. 'Then he does not—' she did not finish the sentence in words, but made a vague, slashing gesture in the vicinity of her own neck.

'I only wish he would,' Gussie sighed.

'Well, my dears,' put in Mrs Jendring, stout, matronly and brisk, as a mother of several daughters ought to be, 'we had better seek out our rooms, had not we? Miss Werth will not wish to be long detained from her escapades.'

'Oh, I *do* hope you will come upon something very horrid!' offered Miss Fanny, as youthful as her sister – a twin, perhaps – and showing it with this girlish effusion of spirits.

'And do tell us all about it, after,' said Miss Cecily.

The eldest Miss Jendring directed a wry look at Gussie, and swept her younger siblings away in a flurry of efficiency. Gussie was soon left to the solitary contemplation of the bloodied and dismembered cherubs adorning the ceiling, and an onward ramble farther into the depths of the house.

'I wonder whether Clarissa has yet arrived,' was her thought as she left the hall. Miss Selwyn would, no doubt, be as enchanted with the Palace of Nightmares as Gussie could be.

APRIL 29TH

The books here are ancient. I attempted to peruse several, only to find them disintegrating in my hands. This is a great pity, for the peculiar notions of prior ages are frequently of interest, as a curiosity if nothing else. It is fortunate that I contrived to bring several of my own volumes in my portmanteau.

Ceaseless revelry was threatened, but as yet nothing at all has happened. I have been at leisure to read as much as I like. I have little hope of being left to such pursuits tomorrow, however.

Great-Uncle Silvester has taken up his abode in my room. I don't know why. He has selected the darkest corner, on the far side of the room to the fireplace, and crouches there near the ceiling, where I cannot get to him. He has not answered me when I have spoken to him. I believe he's sleeping, but he lurks up there in a fashion that seems to bode ill in some indefinable way. As though he stands guard over me.

But I am becoming like Gussie, fanciful and absurd. Surely all is well. We are here for merriment, not murder, though I believe my cousin would enjoy both to a high degree.

I believe I have done. I had little to write, but the book would not let me rest until I had sullied its pages with something or other. It has a way of placing itself in plain sight, where I cannot possibly help catching sight of it, over and over again. To say that it looms *must be ridiculous for so small an article; yet, somehow, it does.*

I shall leave off, and hope to be allowed my peace.

Theo had no expectation of seeking his rest at any early hour, for such was never his habit. But what to do, to while away several hours in a silent house, with nothing to read save those favourite volumes he had brought with him?

Perhaps there might be a dedicated library, elsewhere in the house. A proper, expansive one, well-supplied with tomes in readable condition. Not too much to ask of so large a house, surely?

Theo got out of the deep armchair into which he had sunk, and set aside the little claret-coloured book. He crossed first to the darkest corner of his room, and gazed up at the still, shadowy form crouched aloft. 'Great-Uncle, I am going wandering. Shall you come along?'

The grotesque neither moved nor answered. But, when Theo abandoned the effort to rouse him and moved away, the shadow unfurled itself with a creak of aged stone, and silently winged after.

'Hello,' came a bright voice.

Theo, paused on the threshold of his room, gave a start. The corridor beyond lay empty, he would have said; a single lamp shone on the far wall, leaving much of the space in darkness, but he detected no hint of movement.

'Who's there?' said he, sharply.

'A spirit,' came the answer, in tones of smothered laughter.

Theo sighed. 'Miss Selwyn.'

'I do wish you would call me Clarissa.' The lady, it seemed, had no mind to reveal herself, for she remained hidden. Theo searched the shadows for her slim figure in vain.

'Very well, *Clarissa*,' he growled, contriving to make an insult of the name. 'And what are you doing loitering outside of my room at dead of night?'

'No, is it so late? I had not thought it much past eleven o'clock.'

Theo merely waited, arms folded.

It was her turn to sigh. 'Oh, very well. I came to warn you.'

'Warn me?' Theo's instincts prickled into alertness, mindful as he was of that lurking sense of menace he had been sensible of only moments before.

'They are hunting you.' No laughter now: her tone was deathly serious.

Dread deepened in the pit of Theo's stomach. 'Who? Who are hunting me?'

A pause. 'Miss Appleton, for one,' she mused, incomprehensibly. 'I can say so for a certainty, for she told me of it herself. Miss Weller and Miss Annabel Weller, if I am any judge. One or more of the Jendrings, if they've the stomach for it. Oh, and Miss Malby, *she* would not pass up the opportunity. Mrs Beale, I shouldn't wonder, for her husband has been gone a year and more. Lady Anne Morville – or if not she herself, then her mother on her behalf. In fact, that last goes for a great many young ladies, you ought to be warier of mothers than misses, methinks—'

'*Miss* Selwyn,' Theo interrupted. 'Of what are you talking?'

'You are a grand prize on the marriage mart,' she explained. 'And I thought you were to address me as Clarissa now.'

'The marriage mart.' These words uttered in accents of loathing, Theo could almost have spit with the extent of his disgust.

Clarissa gave an impatient sigh. 'Try to have a little understanding, your lordship. I daresay it is bothersome to you, but you are a man, are not you? Resplendent with all the privilege your sex enjoys, not to mention a handsome income secured for your life. Now consider the plight of the average Miss. We are barred from providing from ourselves, in the way a man could; unwed, we are destined to remain a burden on our brothers and uncles, should we be so fortunate as to possess any wealthy enough to keep us for our lifetimes. Nor may we improve our fortunes by any endeavour of our own, be we ever so clever or hard-working. No, there is only marriage, and forgive me if I point out that it is far more burdensome a predicament to *us* than it can be to you.'

'A pitiable plight, and I sympathise with it,' said Theo, with at least a little truth. 'But I do not choose to make a martyr of myself to the cause.'

'Could not you?' Clarissa's tone turned wheedling. 'We would not expect you to single-handedly resolve every young lady's woes, of course, but *one* you might lift out of want and uncertainty.'

'Yet you came here to warn me, did not you? Presumably to enable me to evade capture.'

'Perhaps I did,' (uttered slyly, half laughingly). 'Perhaps I only wished to gain an advantage over the competition. Consider, Lord Bedgberry. Not Wyrded myself, but a scion of a lusciously Wyrded family – thanks, in part, to your excellent cousin. What young man will have me, save someone such as yourself?'

'No part of that strikes me as my problem.'

A sigh. 'It is Henry's, I suppose. Would that it were only mine.'

Theo, despite himself, felt a flicker of pity, his mind briefly conjuring up an unhappy vision of such helplessness. But Clarissa must not be permitted to sway him; he banished the thought. 'Your duty has been performed,' he said aloud. 'You may now cease bothering me, Miss Selwyn, and permit me to go on with my evening.'

'And where do you go, alone at such an hour?'

'That is my own business.'

'A secret objective, then, and a clandestine escapade. How I envy you.'

'You are not to be invited to join me, however hard you angle for the privilege.'

'Then I must acknowledge defeat, and depart on adventures of my own. I bid you goodnight, your lordship.'

Theo had not needed Clarissa's biting tone to understand her intention. 'And you are not to follow me either.'

'Ah! Well, if you forbid me, then of course I shall not.'

'Of course.' Theo, under no illusions of being obeyed, made a sardonic bow to no one in particular – Clarissa continuing to hide herself from him – and stalked away into the shadows. An irrepressible young lady and a crumbling grotesque followed after, both, perhaps, chuckling to themselves, in their separate ways.

Theo soon forgot the possibility of pursuit. He had not travelled down very many dark passages before he encountered something of interest: an alcove, tucked into a shadowed corner, and nearly missed as he strode along. A dark, bulk of a thing lurked there, bristling with tall, narrow pipes and other paraphernalia: Theo's eyes, adjusting to the gloom, discerned an organ, gleaming faintly silver.

'Curious,' murmured he, pausing. What purpose had an organ in such a house? And in such a spot, too, half-hidden on the way to nowhere in particular.

He stepped nearer – and a note sounded, a deep bass note, reverberating through the floor under Theo's feet.

He stopped at once, his skin prickling with warning. 'Is someone there?' he called.

No one answered him. As the sound died away and silence returned, the pounding of Theo's heart settled, and he advanced again upon the organ.

The note sounded again, along with several more; *loud*, blasting through the hush with sufficient force to wake the whole house.

Theo, for no reason he could have described, began to smile. And then he was up on the little dais and setting his hands to the keys, and from his unknowing fingers flowed forth a resounding melody, no tune he had ever heard before. It rang joyously through the walls and rattled the windows; dust came floating down, from somewhere above.

When, at length, his fingers consented to pause, and permit the rapturous melodies to die away, Theo remained awhile upon the dais, breathing a little hard in the wake of a strange exhilaration.

The silence echoed, louder than ever after so much crashing tumult. A minute or two ticked away before anyone broke it: not with words, but with a low, eldritch chuckle.

'*The Masquerade,*' declared that same, strange voice that had shaken the house upon arrival, '*has begun.*'

There followed a laugh, deep and velvet, raising the hairs upon Theo's neck.

'Right, then,' he muttered, and stepped down from the dais. 'I'll away to bed.'

DAY 1:
MUMMERY

CHAPTER EIGHT

'*The Masquerade has begun!*'

Gussie heard those words proclaimed at a shattering volume, arresting her halfway down an ornate oaken staircase somewhere on the second floor. She had explored the confines of an emerald-upholstered drawing room, and was on her way down, lantern in hand, to inspect a passageway at the bottom, its walls most interestingly lined in tapestries. The organ music had first caused her to hesitate, the triumphant notes drifting in ghostly fashion down abandoned halls and dark corridors, leaving a palpable ripple of *something* in its wake. When the final notes sounded and died away, Gussie perceived a difference: gone was the sense of emptiness, of hushed decay. Now, she felt she was come to an inhabited house; a place of life and laughter, of possibility.

The resonant words electrified her, lent a fizzing energy to her steps. She passed down the remaining stairs with greater purpose, though as devoid of objective as ever. The tapestries seemed to welcome her passage, woven faces both bright and devilish laughing in welcome or mockery. A clock chimed from somewhere within the depths of the house: twelve strikes announcing the turning of the day, resonant and deep with promise.

Then came a babble of conversation, advancing from somewhere ahead. The Jendrings again, perhaps? Gussie strode forth, not at all unwilling to come upon them again – Miss Jendring, the eldest, had perhaps shown some sign of potential as a friend – but she halted after three steps, for something was amiss with her clothing. Accustomed to the fluid sway of muslin as she walked (and she had, that day, chosen to don the best of her gowns, in a lively purple hue), the roll and sway of her garments was entirely *other*, and in every way unfamiliar.

A glance down revealed the utter absence of her gown, or of any recognisable article. She wore gentleman's attire, but of no style she had ever before encountered. Her hips were encased in a short and rather bulbous set of trousers, striped in black and ivory and trimmed in gold braid. A waistcoat of curious fashion matched in fabric and colour, from beneath which emerged long, full sleeves of some cream-coloured cloth. Pale stockings clad her legs, and her feet were resplendent in slippers of ivory and gold.

Best of all, a heavy and sumptuous cape of black, gilded velvet hung from her shoulders, swishing delightfully as she moved. The weight of it seemed to lend her dignity and power; she tried an experimental turn, and revelled in the ponderous sway of the fabric. An answering weight about her brow enlightened her to the presence of a hat, likely adorned with a fascinating plume.

'Why, I am become somebody else altogether,' she said aloud. 'I wonder who?'

There was no time to consider the question, for though the chatter of female voices had died away, someone came around the corner: someone moving fast and heedlessly for he – it was certainly a gentleman – almost collided with her.

'Beg pardon,' said the gentleman hastily, and Gussie recognised Theo.

'Good evening!' she said grandly, pitching her voice deep, and swept him a manly bow.

Theo appeared taken aback, as well he might upon receiving so elaborate a courtesy from a Gussie so handsomely dressed. He returned the bow, perfunctorily, and muttered something about carelessness.

'Theo, do not you know me?' she said, laughingly, but the low timbre of her voice did not fade; she spoke in a handsome baritone.

There was no sign of recognition in Theo's eyes.

'Ought I to?' said he, briefly.

'It's Gussie,' she said, laughing harder, only the words did not emerge as she intended. She had said, 'It is dark,' or perhaps, 'It is late,' for Theo only murmured an uninterested agreement, and excused himself.

Gussie permitted him to go without further attempts to detain him. A tendril of unease stirred within; the disguise, proving more thorough than she could have imagined, might prove very amusing, but why was not she to announce her identity even to her own family? What manner of enchantment prevented her?

The unease grew, and she began to walk, much faster than before. She wanted a looking-glass, in which to examine her face; for she feared her own features were as lost as her own voice, her own clothes.

Here came the Jendrings, then, all in a cluster as before; the music (and the announcement) had drawn everyone forth, of course, and she would soon encounter many strange faces. The ladies gazed upon her in delight, imagining her either a fellow guest – no, her attire must be too strange for that, they thought her part of the masquerade. An entertainer. They curtseyed to her merrily, calling greetings, and seemed inclined to linger, to engage her in conversation.

Gussie made one more attempt. 'You see Miss Werth before you, Miss Jendring. Do not let this curious façade deceive you.'

But this message no more reached Miss Jendring than had her explanation reached Theo. She could not hear how the statement had been twisted as it left her lips, but the ladies all smiled, and Mrs Jendring said: 'To be sure we shall, and thank you sir!'

With which courtesy, they fluttered away, leaving Gussie to continue her breathless search for a mirror unimpeded.

She found one at last, hanging over the fireplace in the seventh or twelfth or hundredth chamber she passed through. The great, lordly thing occupied its extravagant golden frame with pompous elegance, huge and bright and clear: Gussie saw reflected a man, absolutely a man, her own age, perhaps, but in no other way similar. He was tall and handsome and self-assured, with hair and beard of deep auburn, and merry brown eyes. She looked like an old painting in her antiquated attire...

....the thought brought with it a vague recollection: she had passed many a painting in her wanderings through the house, and had not some of those portrayed within them worn garments like these?

Yes, she had seen this man before. He had stepped out of a portrait and come to life: only it was *her* life he had chosen to adopt, muscling her out of it without so much as a by-your-leave.

'Well, and if that is not just like a man,' said Gussie disgustedly. She gave a sigh, feeling very put-out: if she must be subsumed into an involuntary mummer's masquerade, *had* she to wear these absurd trousers?

He carried them well, though, this stranger in the glass. The clothes suited him, as though he wore such garments every day. He probably had, whoever he had been in life.

'Very well, then,' Gussie told the mirror. 'If I am stuck with this seeming, I might as well have a little fun with it.'

APRIL 29TH

Not more than half a night has passed since our arrival in this wretched place and already Gussie is missing.

So says Mama, at least. I cannot find out that anything very out of the way has happened; she is not in her room, that much has been established, but would it be at all like my cousin to retire meekly to bed, like an obedient miss, when there is a great monstrous palace of mysteries to be explored? No indeed! She is flitting about the place somewhere, poking her nose into everything and making a grand nuisance of herself. Depend upon it, that is all that has happened. And if Great-Uncle Silvester and Great-Aunt Honoria cannot locate her, what of that? It means just nothing at all. They are but two, and this house could accommodate a hundred. Nay, two hundred, and perhaps it does, for I have passed a great many other guests in my own wanderings.

It was the organ music that brought them all forth, and I could wish it otherwise. Before that, I was enjoying a solitary ramble, interrupted only by a purposeless interlude with Miss Selwyn. (Her pronouncements were too absurd to set down here, but she has ever been out of her wits).

Why then did I play the thing? I do not even know how to play an organ, haven't touched such an instrument in the whole course of my life. Or any other, for that matter. Something compelled *me, and I would be duly angry save that I found it curiously...enjoyable.*

I couldn't say why. The music swept through me like smoke through clear air, and I felt alight, like a bonfire, or a lantern, or... oh, hell with poetics. I'd play it again now if I dared.

It is probably cursed.

I believe I am being haunted. Perhaps it is something to do with the organ, who can say, but I keep glimpsing a stranger out of the past – when I turn corners, or happen to glance back. Soft footsteps echoing behind me, and only a flicker of brocade when I attempt to discover who it is... only once have I come face-to-face with the shade, and full strange he was, dressed in outlandish attire all in black, ivory and gold. I came upon a portrait of him, oh, it must have been two or even three hundred years old. That face smiled at me in seeming welcome, then the impudent fellow bowed in a manner all mockery.

Who he is, or why he should have taken to tormenting me, I cannot say. I am determined to catch him at it, and when I do...

It had been a night for strange occurrences – and compulsions, the first having struck Theo as he stepped up to the organ, the second coming upon him as he ducked through a low doorway to evade a gaggle of laughing guests bearing relentlessly down upon him. The room beyond the door proved to be a study carrel, or some such thing, for it bore a desk and chair of some dark, almost black, wood. Someone had lit a lantern, filling the room with an inviting, mellow glow, and a tapestried rug lay thrown over the flagstone floor. No sooner had Theo set eyes upon that ancient-looking desk than he knew he had to employ it: the journal required attention.

More than that, it required *words.*

The urge to write struck him like an insistent itch, and would not ease until he had taken up pen and ink and scrawled his few paragraphs onto the next blank, white page.

He sighed as he returned the little journal to his pocket. It had him in its grip, the deceptively unassuming volume. He ought, perhaps, to have investigated the thing more thoroughly before ever he had written a word.

It was too late now.

Clarissa lay in wait for him outside the door, lounging against the opposite wall. 'I cannot find Gussie,' she hissed as he emerged. 'And you are being followed.'

'By you, it appears,' muttered Theo. She was dressed oddly again, rather like the footwomen who had escorted his family to the masquerade. Exactly like them, in fact; whose livery had she mercilessly stolen?

'Yes, but also someone else,' Clarissa insisted. 'A man, wearing the oddest clothes I ever saw, and if I am not much mistaken he is come out of a painting hereabouts.'

Theo merely nodded, and moved past her.

'Well! I thought at least to interest you a little with such news as that,' she complained, trailing after.

'Not very.'

'Where are you going?'

Theo had no answer for that, being equally without destination or desire to impart it to Miss Selwyn. 'Where is your brother?' he said instead. 'Wherever he is, there is Gussie like to be.'

'You mean Henry?' Clarissa appeared startled. 'You think Gussie will go to him?'

'No,' snarled Theo. 'I think he will go to Gussie.'

Clarissa pondered that, unabashed. 'You may be right,' she decided, and left him without another word.

Theo glanced back, but saw no signs of further pursuit – either by Clarissa, or by the mysterious gentleman from the portrait. He hastened his steps anyway. He was unused to so much company, at any time; let alone in the earliest hours after midnight, when the world usually lay dark in slumber. Perhaps he ought simply to retire to his own room, read away the remainder of the night, and leave everybody else to rattle around like a flock of chickens, if they would.

Before he could act on this amiable thought, the great, hulking shape of some giant, or possibly ogre, appeared from around a corner and barrelled towards him. Theo swiftly recognised Ballantine, moving at speed and evidently ill at ease, and sighed. 'Yes, what is it?' he said testily as the ogre drew level with him.

Ballantine stopped, and blinked at him in surprise. 'Pardon me,' he said, with a cursory bow. He looked Theo over in silence for a moment, and then added, 'Perhaps I mistake the matter, but you may be someone who can answer a question for me.'

Theo, his mood souring further by the moment, merely raised his brows, and waited.

'Just what the devil is going on?' said Ballantine.

Theo's brows rose further. 'How the devil should I know?'

'Forgive me, I thought you must be...' The Runner trailed off, and bowed sharply. 'Pardon me,' he said again, and passed on down the corridor.

Theo enjoyed several moments of befuddled feelings. Mr. Ballantine's behaviour was strange indeed, and something seemed amiss with Theo himself. His voice had come out oddly, his words pitched a little deeper than usual. His face itched around the chin. And he was wearing a hat?

He groped at his head: yes, a velvet confection with a plume perched there.

He looked down, and saw: black, midnight blue, and silver; short, rounded trousers and hose; a skirted tunic of some sort; a codpiece. A codpiece!

His face *itched*; he scratched it, and his fingers encountered a beard.

Theo stood for some moments stock-still in confusion. 'How is it,' he asked the empty air, 'that I am become my own pursuer?'

For he had taken on the semblance of that same bearded fellow from the portrait, the one who had been following him for an hour or more. Stay, no; that attire had been gold-gilded, and there was none on Theo's garments. Not the same, then, but similar enough.

No wonder Ballantine had behaved oddly. Perhaps he thought Theo was in some way affiliated with the masquerade, and might be able to elucidate the madness.

'Not a bit of it,' Theo sighed. How in the blazes was he to get out of this fellow's skin again? He had no notion how he had got *into* it in the first place.

And what the devil had become of Gussie, anyway? For if *he* could transform into another person without knowing anything about it, then so could she...

He turned, scanning the shadowy passageway behind him. 'I know who you are!' he shouted.

He waited, but nobody emerged, and nobody spoke. If it was Gussie, then, she had given up on him, and gone off to haunt somebody else.

Well, and good. He was off to bed.

He paused, though, and cast another long look at his own frame so strangely clad. He did not look in the least like himself.

And, curiously, he did not feel in the least like himself.

'I don't have to be me,' he realised. Not Theodore Werth, Lord Bedgberry, bachelor under pursuit (according to Clarissa). Not Theo, out of place and out of patience no matter where he went.

He could be – someone else. Someone tall and bearded and from another era altogether. Someone bold and unburdened.

His mind returned, briefly and surprisingly, to Clarissa in her stolen livery. Was this why she was so rarely to be found in a gown, as she ought to be? He recalled the freedom with which she'd turned from him and wandered away upon business of her own, with the swinging stride of unabashed confidence.

Well, then. Perhaps she was onto a good thing.

Theo felt a smile come to his lips. He paused to take his bearings, and then – when he had determined in which approximate direction that wonderful organ lay – he turned his steps towards it, and strode away.

In fact, it would be fairer to say that he *swaggered*.

CHAPTER NINE

GUSSIE HAD INDEED ABANDONED the haunting of Theo, but not because some stray and uncharacteristic stab of conscience had assailed her. No; she had merely caught sight of a more tempting target for torment, a target gigantic in size and ogre-shaped.

What Ballantine was doing in his ogre aspect when the party was but just beginning, Gussie could not guess. Typically, he adopted his Wyrded guise only at times of need, and – considering the sheer might and brawn of him – those times usually consisted of some danger.

She did not *think* anyone was likely to have got into peril already, but still, there was an ogre on the loose; what did he know that she did not?

Irresistible question. She plunged after him, forgetting Theo in an instant.

She passed the Jendrings going one way, her aunt going the other; Lady Alicia Greaves, luxuriously draped, with Mrs Bidden trailing in her wake; Charles Selwyn; several other ladies and gentlemen she did not know; and, excitingly, two or three others, like herself, in strange array. These last were almost enough to distract her from her quest: one gentleman wore the long, dark curls and wide-brimmed hat of a cavalier, decked in velvet and lace down to his high-heeled shoes. A lady wore the wide panniers of the previous century, fully five feet at the hip if she was an inch, with her hair powdered white and stacked dangerously high.

Who were they, and where were they going? She could follow only one of these tempting mysteries, and though she wavered each time some new, sumptuously dressed stranger sailed by her (and more so when, on occasion, they stopped, and curtseyed or bowed to her, and asked her, half-laughingly, how she did), she remained in pursuit of the Bow Street Runner.

She found Goodspeed before she caught up with Ballantine – or perhaps he had found *her*, for he looked directly at her in all her borrowed regalia and said: 'Ah, Miss Werth.'

Gussie had not felt the illusion descend upon her, but she felt its departure: a cold, slithering sensation, as though her skin had oozed away. Unpleasant: she shivered. 'Mr Goodspeed,' she answered tartly, shaking out the restored folds of her skirts. 'I was not yet finished.'

'My apologies, miss,' he said with a brief bow. 'If you were to share the nature of your errand, perhaps I may assist.'

'I was wreaking havoc and mischief upon unwary kinsmen.'

Goodspeed nodded in perfect understanding. Before he could answer, Great-Aunt Honoria's head swooped into sudden view, causing Gussie to jump back. 'Ah!' she crowed. 'Gussie! Ivo, I have found her! At *last*.'

Ivo's face appeared, wreathed in smiles. 'Your poor aunt is beside herself with concern,' he said, beaming.

At that moment, Lady Werth was seated in peaceful solitude in a small breakfast-parlour in the west wing of the house, sipping a glass of sherry and perusing a slim volume of poetry. Since these facts were equally unknown to Ivo Farthing and Gussie alike, the pronouncement was permitted to pass unchallenged.

'Now you may tell her I am well,' said Gussie with some impatience. 'And then Mr. Goodspeed will restore my disguise, and I shall be on my way.'

'I'm afraid I cannot, miss,' said Goodspeed. 'It is a Mummer's Dance, you see.'

Gussie did not. She looked at her Great-Aunt for elucidation.

'Oh, I know nothing of it, my dear!' declared Honoria. 'It was no part of the masquerade before, that ever I heard.'

'Then how do you know about it?' said Gussie to Goodspeed, who, smoothly ignoring the question, only smiled a little.

'Some of the guests are appointed as mummers,' he explained. 'Disguised, it is their task to harry the remainder, unless and until somebody guesses their identity. Then the masquerade is finished.'

'Harrying!' said Gussie, throwing up her hands. 'There, you see! Cheated out of half my mischief, and I am such a natural at it.'

Great-Aunt Honoria had lost interest. Goodspeed had halted Gussie's progress in the midst of a rather large music-room, draped in indigo velvets and replete with musical accoutrements of every sort. Honoria manifested hands, the better to catch up and sport with a raucous set of pipes. She did not appear to possess any natural talent for melody.

'The game is only changed, miss,' offered Goodspeed. 'Now you may put your wits to the test, and seek to uncover the identities of the remaining mummers. Little can daunt your skills there, I should imagine.'

Gussie had the lurking feeling that she was being managed, and skilfully at that. 'Perhaps that would be appealing,' she could not but allow. 'Though I do not know most of the guests here. That must be an obstacle to success.'

'It is all a matter of asking the right questions.' Goodspeed bowed to Gussie, and only as he turned his back and left the music-room did it occur to her that his attire, too, had altered. He was not wearing the neat, sober-coloured garments which so befit his position in her family's household. His attire more nearly resembled that of the black-and-silver clad footwomen, without the hat.

Curious.

'Come, Aunt! We are going mummering!' called Gussie cheerfully, and plunged back into the fray.

She had, in the midst of her conversation with the butler, forgotten all about Mr Ballantine.

THE AFORESAID MR. BALLANTINE, the while, did *not* enjoy the whirl of chaos unleashed upon the house by the strange, resonant notes of the organ. Everyone had promptly lost their wits, he concluded, for he could hardly move a step before bumping into some half-drunk soul scurrying hither and yon, shrieking fit to burst with mirth, and making a great nuisance of themselves. There was not even any punch being served, no claret, no ratafia. The guests were drunk on something else; mischief perhaps, or magic, or mystery, or some dangerous concoction of them all.

He had not meant to take up his ogrish shape, had scarcely noted that he had done so. It had happened after, or more probably during, the organ's riotous parade of music, as though the transcendent, trumpeting melody had in some manner stirred up his Wyrde.

It had probably stirred up everybody's Wyrde.

He had not, since, found it possible to calm himself enough to return to his regular form. The chaos was too acute, the whirl too muddling, the noise too deafening. The circumstances were perfect, he thought, for a less innocent sort of mischief: if the jewel-thief he sought was here, then he or she would find themselves with a tempting array of valuables on offer, and more than sufficient opportunity to claim them.

Someone was playing the organ again, he realised distantly. The soaring melody struggled to make itself heard over the tumult of revelry, but not for lack of trying. Whoever was playing was doing so with emphasis and vigour, and since the effect was to drive the guests to greater excesses, Ballantine could cheerfully have throttled them.

The music called to the ogre in his blood in some strange and eldritch way; under its fell influence, Ballantine drew himself up to his fullest height and *roared*.

He had wandered into a ballroom, where some few couples were attempting to waltz along to the demented clamour of the music. The ogre's bellow cut through even their fervour; the sound rattled the walls, and brought the dancers and their spectators to a shocked halt.

Abashed, Ballantine wished himself smaller again, human again, but without effect. His Wyrde had got him in its grip and had no mind to release him. He growled an apology and retreated, veering towards a beckoning door.

On the other side he found an elegant salon all in yellow silk, occupied by three people: a lady he recognised as Lady Alicia Greaves; an unknown gentleman just disappearing through a far door; and a strange vision of a woman in the extravagant ermine and velvet of a Tudor queen, her dark hair dressed with jewels.

The scene seemed innocent enough; he could not have said what it was about the latter lady that aroused his suspicions.

Perhaps it was the mildness with which she beheld the approach of the ogre that he was, not a trace of the surprise or shock or even fear to which he was accustomed. True, she may simply be of a Wyrded family boasting an ogre or two among its members, and as such was quite used to it. But something about her tugged at his attention.

'My goodness,' said Lady Alicia, examining him closely. 'Is this the famous Bow Street Runner? I have heard such tales of you, young man.'

'That is mutual, my lady,' he said with a brief bow, much to Lady Alicia's delight.

The Tudor queen heard this with a strange flicker of a smile, and in another instant she was gone, darting soundlessly out of the room before Ballantine could detain her.

'Who was that woman?' Ballantine demanded.

'I am sure I do not know,' answered Lady Alicia, her words a little slurred. Was she drunk, or was it merely the strange effects of the music and the manor?

Ballantine looked hard at her. 'Are you well, ma'am?'

'Perfectly!' said she with excellent cheer. 'I do seem to have lost something, now let me see, what was it...' She proceeded to examine her clothing, without much effect; a patting of her pockets and a turning-out of her reticule resulted in no enlightenment.

Ballantine, observing the bare, white expanse of her throat, received a premonition. 'It was not jewels, perhaps, was it?' said he with a sinking sense of foreboding.

'That was it!' she agreed, and slumped, unsteadily, onto a striped divan. 'But I cannot remember which I put *on* this evening. It may have been the diamonds, or perhaps—'

Ballantine did not stay to hear the remainder of her wonderings; he was out the door already, running in pursuit of the Tudor queen. There had been that degree of slyness to her expression, and a something odd in her gaze when Lady Alicia had uttered those words: *Bow Street Runner.* Not wariness; nothing so straightforward. An energy, an interest: as though a game had begun, and she was in no way loath to compete.

That she had deprived the befuddled, Wyrde-addled Lady Alicia of her jewels seemed indubitable to Ballantine. But who *was* she? Who were *they*, these characters out of time? For he had glimpsed others in his wanderings, and he saw more of them now, barrelling as he was through knots of chattering people in vain pursuit of the fugitive. A gentleman in the dress of a Jacobean courtier; a pair of children, twins, clad in holly-green velvet and lace; a fair-haired lady who would not have been out of place at the Court of Marie Antoinette. He did not believe they were guests, or not in the ordinary way. Their appearance was too good, too exact. These were not costumes worn by giggling ladies and self-conscious gentlemen. They were paintings come to life.

And yet, one of them was the jewel-thief.

He could not make sense of it, but he hardly needed to. For the present, he only needed to catch the Tudor queen. Questions may then be posed, and mysteries resolved – but luck did not favour him, for he needed very few minutes to discover that the chaos and the crowds had swallowed up the lady, as thoroughly as though she had never been.

'A lady passed this way,' he said, to those whose revelries barred his way. 'Dressed all in velvet, with pearls at her throat, and dark hair. A queen from long ago. Have you seen her?'

No one had, or no one would own that they had. He was obliged at last to abandon the chase, balked of his prey; a loser in the game. He retired disgruntled, befuddled. What was afoot? Had the jewel-thief merely taken advantage of the reigning clamour to exercise their talents under the obscuring camouflage of a lucky disguise? Or was something worse at work? Was the masquerade itself, and those who held it, part of the scheme?

He hoped the former might prove the truth; then he faced only one opponent, though a resourceful and clever one. He was a match for that much, he trusted.

If the latter, he faced several thieves, united in a much grander scheme. Whoever had called the masquerade possessed wealth and grandeur beyond counting, besides a sumptuous Wyrde bordering upon the magical. How was he to counter such concerted advantages as that – even with the help of the Werths?

His comfort must be, that anybody so replete with money and status had no need of more. What motive could they have for divesting their fellows of mere jewels – however valuable? No, he must be mistaken in thinking it.

He needed quiet to clear his head; the chaos was muddling his thoughts. Gradually, pushing his way through knots of chattering people and drunken dancers, he sought some sign of a staircase: one leading down, by preference. There was no food on offer at this strange parade, not yet. The kitchens, then, were like to prove the quietest place in the house, provided no other guests had come to the same idea.

He found a way down at last, tucked into a corner behind a billiard room, at the end of a long, richly carpeted passage. Blessed dimness beckoned, a cessation of the bright, almost blinding lights of a thousand beeswax candles set into a thousand elaborate sconces. He charged that way, stumbled down; the riotous noise lessened, and finally ceased. Even the demented strains of the distant organ dampened to a whisper.

Ballantine slumped against a white-washed wall, breathing hard. No fires were lit; the chill seeped through his clothes, and he welcomed the sensation after the clammy heat of too many bodies, too many candles, too much excitement, that prevailed above stairs.

Slowly, he calmed, and in doing so, shifted. His frame shrank in height and bulk, returned to its ordinary proportions, and he sighed, softly, in relief. There was a strain to his ogre shape, a feeling of... not wrongness, for it was as natural a shape to him as his own, human limbs. A jarring sense of *being* wrong, of being unsuited to the world around him; of being too big, too tall, too strong, too terrifying. Even here, in this mass of Wyrded wonders, did he feel it.

In all the Wyrde-addled revellers who had crossed his path this evening, still he had seen no other ogre.

He had encountered plenty of shocked amazement, plenty of apprehension. Glances had slid away from him, then returned, wide-eyed; fascinated, appalled.

In truth, if he valued nothing else about the Werths he must value their coolness, their unflappability. Only they had ever regarded him without fear or concern, no matter how he towered over them when in the grip of his Wyrde. They regarded him with a total absence of any particular interest, in point of fact: with near total *indifference*, for what was a mere ogre in the midst of their extravagantly Wyrded ranks?

The Tudor queen, the thief. *She* had not experienced any sensation of terror or alarm, either. *She* had beheld him with interest, with some strange alacrity, and this, too, he found remarkable. Compelling. He pursued her because he must; she had broken the law, and he was sworn to enact the King's justice in punishment.

Were he to consider the matter with frank honesty, here in the silence of his own soul, he was bound to admit: he also pursued her because he was fascinated. A mere momentary glance had done thus much. Who was she? He had to know.

He became aware of a soft sound penetrating the blanketing silence below. He had paused halfway down a featureless passage, white-walled and cold, the floor bare stone and emanating a frigid chill. The stairs back to life and revelry lay shadowed in the dimness to his right; to his left, there was only impenetrable darkness. The kitchen, most like. He could hear someone moving around, stealthily: soft, slow steps, as though hopeful of evading notice.

Perhaps they could hear him, too.

He rose from his half-slumped posture. He could retrace his steps, return upstairs, and avail himself of one of the many bright candles burning in branched sconces along the walls; catch up an oil lantern, perhaps, for he had seen a great many of those, too, stationed upon console tables or hanging from hooks in the ceiling. Thus armed, he would see the stealthy intruder in plenty of time to determine an appropriate course of action.

But they would also be warned of his approach, and might, therefore, evade him. His eyes had adjusted somewhat to the darkness, and dim shapes had emerged from the deep shadows: enough, at least, to avoid blundering into a wall, or falling over a footstool.

He turned to his left, and advanced, as soft-footed and stealthy as his quarry could be.

Before he had gone very far, someone came barrelling towards him, a flurry of frenzied movement that took him by surprise. A body collided with his: his arms, suddenly, were full of female warmth, the softness of skin and silk, a gentle fragrance assailing his senses.

This being so utterly other than anything he had expected or imagined, Ballantine froze.

A stabbing pain brought him out of his stasis with a jerk, and a sharp cry. His neck. Someone had stabbed his neck. With their *teeth*. She'd bitten him, the wretch, bitten him until his blood flowed and she was *drinking it—*

'Oh dear,' said she in a trembling voice, though without withdrawing either her body from his grasp or her mouth from his bloodied throat. 'I am so sorry – no manners at all, Mama always said it of me – you see I am so *hungry—*' and this, apparently, being explanation and apology enough (in the lady's view) she returned to her repast without further remark.

'Hold on,' Ballantine blurted, attempting to push her away, but she was like a limpet, or an octopus – all arms, and clinging. 'Wait a moment, if you please, that hurts—'

'Sorry,' she muttered, gulping blood.

'I would advise you to desist, madam, or we shall both regret it,' he warned, but she would not be deterred, and under such treatment as *that* the result was inevitable.

The transformation hurt, sometimes, when it came upon him too quickly. It was that which caused him to bellow, not rage, and he felt a little ashamed when (at last) she released him, and staggered back. He could not see her face clearly in the near darkness, but a shocked gasp from her bespoke alarm.

'Oh, dear,' she said faintly. 'I *am* sorry.'

'I did try to warn you,' sighed Ballantine. Ogre-Wyrded, and twice in an hour. The masquerade was not beginning well.

'I suppose you will kill me now,' said the lady regretfully. 'And I can hardly blame you, for I shall owe it all to my own carelessness.'

'You shall,' Ballantine agreed. 'That, and a disgraceful lack of ordinary courtesy. Could you not at least have asked before you savaged me?'

'I could have,' she admitted. 'But people usually say no, you see, and I was very hungry.'

'I cannot think why anyone would decline so pleasant an experience.' He bit off each word, feeling savage himself. His neck hurt, and a thin stream of blood ran and ran down his throat; his coat would be ruined.

He chose to interpret the ensuing silence as a show of regret on the lady's part.

'Well,' he said with another sigh. 'I should complain to the establishment about the lack of ready refreshment, if I were you. It was not unreasonable to expect some manner of repast attending the festivities.'

'Are you not going to kill me?' she asked, with friendly interest.

'I should,' he growled. 'But I won't.'

'I'm sure I am very much obliged to you.'

'That makes me feel a great deal better.'

He felt, rather than saw her smile, some near-imperceptible lightening of the tension. 'I suppose it is a little too late to be introducing myself.'

'I would like you to do so, however. Then I may know who to avoid in the future.'

She accepted this remark without comment. 'I am Miss Jendring.' A whisper of fabric and a slight shifting of the shadows informed him that there'd been a curtsey, even if he could not see it.

'Charmed,' he said shortly. 'I am Hugh Ballantine.'

'May I entreat you not to mention this lapse of mine to Mamma? Only there will be a scene, and a lecture, and I should not like to inconvenience her so much. She is here to enjoy herself, after all.'

'Very considerate of you, Miss Jendring.'

'It is, rather.'

'I might be so good as not to mention it,' he allowed. 'But I will require something in return.'

'Oh,' said the lady.

'When you were so good as to throw yourself upon my neck, you interrupted me in pursuit of a person I have reason to imagine is a thief.'

'Oh!' said the lady. 'But you do not imagine she is down here? No one has come this way in the last quarter of an hour, except yourself.'

'No, I had already failed to intercept her. I came down those stairs in hope of a moment's peace.'

'But whatever for?'

'I had some idea of enjoying an interlude of productive thought.'

'You mean that you were angry, and came down here to talk yourself into a better humour.'

'Something like that,' he admitted.

'You don't sound angry now.'

'If I'm not, I ought to be.'

'I shall make amends,' promised Miss Jendring. 'You may rely on me.'

'An experienced thief-taker, are you?'

'No,' came the cheerful answer. 'But I am like to become very bored without an occupation to amuse me, and my sisters say I am insufferable in such a state.'

Ballantine had come to regret having ever mentioned the subject of the thief. What could have possessed him? This girl – for everything about her spoke of youth and frivolity – could have no skills or arts of any relevance to employ, and for those investigations requiring either rank or femininity, he had already secured assistance. Besides, he feared he had been indiscreet. It would serve him right if she turned out to be a chattering gossip.

The shock to his nerves must have been greater than he had supposed, not to mention the loss of no small quantity of blood. He shook his head to clear it, without much effect, and sighed.

'I believe I shall leave off loitering in the shadows with unaccompanied young ladies, and return to the festivities,' he said, without much enthusiasm.

'Oh dear, is it very dark? I suppose it must be.' Miss Jendring walked past him on her way to the stairs; he followed.

She saw clearly in the dark, then; an advantage Ballantine had often wished he possessed. She moved quickly, as though determined to outpace even his lengthy stride. As she disappeared up the stairs, some way ahead of him, Ballantine glimpsed, in the returning glow of the candles, a vision of fair-haired youth clad in ice-blue silk, her angel's face liberally bloodied with gore.

Well, thought he. In an assembly such as this, so shocking an appearance would scarcely occasion any remark.

CHAPTER TEN

LET US RETURN TO the inimitable Miss Werth, and her predations upon the hapless and unsuspecting mummers. If Miss
Jendring, uniting an angelic appearance with youthful good
cheer, tended to win confidence without either effort or merit,
Gussie's advantages were scarcely less. Deceptively obliging in
manner, and smiling with enjoyment, she made no small degree
of progress in the game.

The assistance, if such it could be termed, of Great-Aunt
Honoria and Ivo Farthing proved more hindrance than help.
Still, they made a merry trio of inquisitors. A clock somewhere
struck two; Gussie wondered, distantly, that she was not yet
tired. In truth, she felt overfilled with energy, positively fizzing
with it.

A gentleman in an overlong embroidered waistcoat and extravagant hat had early defeated them – 'You are a person I
never met in the whole course of my life, I am sure,' Gussie had
decided, after eight or ten questions had done naught but bring
a smile of amusement to the cavalier's face, and no enlighten-

ment. But he was a tiresome fellow; Gussie abandoned him with alacrity.

The twins, also, proved beyond her skill to guess: she was acquainted with no children of their age, save Nell's, and Nell was not here. She would have passed them by, save that they accosted her, twirling in their holly-green velvet, and demanded that she make the attempt.

'For you will never guess, I am sure!' declared one of them. Nothing would have given Gussie greater satisfaction than to squash such unseemly glee at once, and without hesitation, but sadly the child proved correct: away they ran again, laughing, to madden somebody else.

'Impertinent,' Gussie declared. '*I* can never have been so trying to the patience.'

'At what age?' mused Great-Aunt Honoria. 'As a child, to be sure, you were so well-behaved, your poor aunt imagined you a changeling, or a haunt. But thankfully that did not last beyond a year or two.'

'Who has been impertinent?' said somebody else, before Gussie could reply to this fresh outrage. She turned, and beheld: the tallest man she had ever seen (excepting only Mr. Ballantine, when he had his ogrishness upon him). He was mummering, there could not be two opinions about that, for in splendour he fair outshone the king and all his court together. His garb was out of distant history, doublet, hose and all; a flat-topped cap in sapphire velvet matched his cape; his shoes bore pearls and beads of gold, and jewels dripped from his fingers and his ears.

Ermine and cloth-of-gold, velvet and silk: he was a feast for the eyes, and with a comely countenance, too. Gussie stared.

He smiled, with a trace of uncertainty: this one was unused either to the splendour or the comeliness, then. 'Miss Werth,' he said, and bowed, taking off his cap with a flourish. Beneath, his hair was a mass of auburn curls, and his eyes crinkled when he smiled. The effect was congenial, if misleading: he could be anybody under that handsome façade.

Great-Aunt Honoria's head descended, swoopingly, in a flurry of smoke. 'Oh! Oh! This one knows us, Gussie. I do believe we have a chance!'

'Lady Honoria,' said the mummer, with another, still more elaborate bow.

Gussie subjected him to a narrow-eyed scrutiny, her suspicions aroused. 'I know who you are,' she announced.

He appeared crestfallen. 'Already? I had not known myself to be so transparent.'

'There is only one gentleman I know who could unite so sumptuous and handsome an appearance with such exquisite courtesy, not to mention diffidence.'

'Perhaps I am not a gentleman,' he suggested gently.

'Or a man at all,' Gussie mused. 'Yes, that might throw out my theory. Very well, I must investigate further.'

'Please, say on,' said the mummer, with that smile.

'Have we been acquainted with each other very long?'

'An unfair question,' said he promptly, 'for "short" and "long" are relative terms. I should call it an acquaintance of respectable length, but perhaps you will think differently.'

'Evasive, Mr Mummer.'

'Is that not a part of the game?'

Gussie harrumphed. 'Very well, I proceed. Are you a man?'

'A direct hit!' Great-Aunt Honoria enthused. 'Though perhaps too direct, my dear. A mystery must not be uncovered *too* quickly, or there is scarce any enjoyment in it.'

'And we must give the poor gentleman a chance,' put in Ivo.

Gussie only awaited her opponent's response, smiling.

'I am a man,' he allowed.

'Ah. But are you a man *generally*? Not just in the present moment, by way of disguise.'

He chuckled. 'I am used to the gentlemanly state, yes.'

Gussie sighed. 'I believe you are right, Honoria. If the game is too easy, there can only be dullness and insipidity.'

'Who am I, then?' said the mummer.

'You are Henry, Lord Maundevyle, and I knew it from the first moment you smiled at me.'

The illusion shimmered, and melted away: there stood Lord Maundevyle, wearing an expression that seemed undecided between gratified and chagrined. 'It seems paltry to be so easily seen through,' he said, rueful. 'Is it so memorable a smile, however?'

'Yes,' said Gussie shortly, in answer to one or perhaps both comments, she hardly knew. 'You should not have approached me, my lord, if you wanted to evade discovery a while longer.'

'But I saw you, and could not resist.'

Gussie received this without remark, and only sighed. 'Well, you must make amends by joining our investigative company. There remain several mummers yet to be unmasked, I believe.'

'Clarissa is among them,' Henry offered. 'So I surmise, for I have seen nothing of her these past two hours.'

It was not like Clarissa Selwyn to hide herself away while so much revelry was going on, indeed. Gussie's spirits rose in an instant. 'There! We shall make it our mission to discover her, and ruin all her amusements. I rely on you, Lord Maundevyle, for you must know your sister best.'

His lordship did not appear to share her confidence in his superior knowledge of his sister's likely escapades; his mouth twisted, and a brow rose. 'You do not imagine it to lie within the power of any mere mortal to anticipate Clarissa?'

'I cannot disagree with your logic,' Gussie answered. 'Well then, we will have to trust to fate to guide us, for no fair forces of destiny would deny me the satisfaction of divesting her of her disguise.'

Henry merely bowed. Great-Aunt Honoria had disappeared somewhere again, leaving the venture under Gussie's sole direction; she looked about herself, and thought.

Where *might* Clarissa go, indeed? What might she do, when so unwisely granted the power of anonymity?

Anywhere, anything. There could be no discovering her through sense or reason; it would have to be through chaos. 'We will go this way,' she decided and set off.

She had accosted Lord Maundevyle in the midst of a large salon, an oval room with a high, arched ceiling elaborately painted with storm clouds and shadows. Two women sat giggling upon a velvet divan; a matron in emerald silk slumped in an armchair near the hearth, singing softly under her breath; a gentleman in knee-breeches chased a laughing girl from one door to the other, and vanished from the room.

Gussie followed the frolicsome pair, finding them by far the liveliest of the company. Beyond the salon, she discovered a study, or something like it: two or three round mahogany tables sat about, flanked by high-backed chairs clad in ocean-blue velvet, a quantity of pens and paper provided for the use of guests. A letter-writing room? But to whom might one write from so strange a place, and how would a missive ever be sent?

Gussie passed through the room without pausing, entering a corridor beyond. Double doors opened up on her left; a card-room, with several gentlemen already engaged in challenging each other's intellect, and striving to empty their opponent's pockets of valuables.

There was one lady present also: a tall, handsome woman, regal in posture, and dressed in a striking black velvet gown trimmed in ermine. She was not out of any recent period of history; hers was the attire of ages long past, and Gussie's interest was instantly arrested.

'A mummer!' she declared, and stopped on the threshold. She watched the woman's doings a moment in silence, for she was no mere idle observer of the games. She walked from table to table – no, *walked* was too tame a term; she strutted, slunk with the boneless grace of a cat – and as she passed each gentleman she touched something about them: corrected the sit of a hat, adjusted a cravat, or merely laid her hand upon a shoulder.

Her progress distracted more than one player from his game: many eyes were fastened upon her, and well they might be, for she could only be described as dazzling.

'There are two possibilities here, that come to mind,' she observed to Henry in a low voice. 'Either we perceive your disgraceful sister enjoying herself far too well; or we may have another mesmerist on our hands.'

'My fervent hope is for the former,' Henry said.

'Mine also,' she agreed. 'But I suspect not. Clarissa is an imp. This woman is a predator.' She advanced upon the card-players, and contrived to place herself directly in the queenly woman's path. 'Good evening,' she said, with a savage smile Clarissa herself would have been proud of.

Cool grey eyes surveyed her with an infuriating glint of amusement. 'Do you come to play?'

'I am playing.' Gussie smiled. 'But not at cards.'

The woman wore jewels to put Queen Elizabeth's to shame, enormous garnets and diamonds set in silver and gold. Somehow such finery only offset her handsomeness, granting her stature, importance; any other woman (Gussie included) would have faded away under them. Her hair, too, was reddish-blonde. She could almost have been the Virgin Queen come to life.

Gussie endured a brief stab of envy. Short, puffy trousers and a codpiece for her, and this woman was a queen! She sighed inwardly.

'You intrigue me,' said her majesty, with that mocking look.

'I am engaged in the Mummer's Dance, and I am here to win a victory over you,' Gussie said, as coolly as she could.

Beside her, Henry snorted with laughter. Gussie ignored him.

'Very well then, I accept your questions,' said the queen. Their conversation had drawn the attention of most of the room: few of the gentlemen remained absorbed by their card-games, and instead watched Gussie and her opponent. She had the uncomfortable feeling that they were, all of them, ranged on the side of the queen.

Gussie would be cowed by nothing, including a roomful of scornful gentry. She folded her arms, and subjected her smirking majesty to a withering stare. 'Do you know who I am?'

It occurred to her to wonder whether it was possible to lie, while under the influence of the Mummer's guise; it had not entered Gussie's head to attempt it, during her turn. By the wary look on the queen's face, perhaps not, for surely she would have lied rather than say, so grudgingly, 'I do.'

'Have we met before?' Gussie pressed. 'Or do you know me by reputation only.'

'I have seen you. You may not have seen me.'

Gussie pondered. Illuminating questions, as far as they went; but then, her circle of acquaintance had expanded somewhat of late, having attended evening parties under her aunt's care. She might have overlooked any number of people.

'Did you see me in London?' Gussie persevered, hoping to narrow down the pool of possible suspects; the queen hesitated, her gaze turning wary, and Gussie's hopes rose—

A clamour went up somewhere near at hand, a cacophony of deep, resonant strikes upon a chorus of gongs.

'Dinner is served,' said the queen, and with a crooked smirk of a smile, she was gone.

'I do not feel that went as well as it could have,' Gussie confided to Henry, as the gentlemen around them abandoned their cards and pursued their queen to the dining-parlour.

'It was a valiant effort,' Lord Maundevyle offered.

'I do seem to be hungry,' Gussie said in reply, and drifted towards the door.

It was Henry who, after a brief silence, said: 'A moment, Miss Werth.' He stopped her on the threshold, and swept a frowning gaze over her, from head to toe and back up again. 'Were you not wearing jewels?'

Suddenly alarmed, Gussie groped at her neckline. Smooth, bare skin – and nothing more. 'My pearls! I was wearing Mama's pearls.' She gasped in horror, and directed a look of pure venom in the direction the queen had gone. 'That awful woman!'

'It may have been her,' Henry allowed. 'But I admit, I cannot recall whether you still had the pearls when we entered this room.'

Gussie sighed: neither, in honesty, could she. Whoever had taken her pearls had abstracted them so lightly, so undetectably, the deed could have been committed at any time this past hour. And what a quantity of people had she encountered in that time!

CHAPTER ELEVEN

S<small>OMEONE WAS SPEAKING.</small>

Whoever it was failed to make themselves heard over the thundering majesty of the organ for some time; Theo only became aware of his company when the lady (for lady it was) so far forgot her dignity as to raise her dulcet voice to a blistering roar.

'*Excuse me*, sir!'

The music ceased, instantly, lingering echoes hanging in the air. Theo turned. 'Madam,' he said frostily. 'I perceive there is something with which I may assist you.'

'Say rather, there is something with which I may assist *you*. Dinner is being served, sir, and you were playing so loudly as to miss the gongs.' She paused, and thought it helpful to add, 'There was quite the chorus of them, too.'

She was a young thing, with a hopeful smile and a quantity of light hair arranged into ringlets. An ice-blue gown clothed her long limbs; Theo noted in passing that someone had spilled rather a lot of blood on it. 'I don't eat,' he said, briefly, and turned back to his organ.

'Oh! Well, that's all right then.' Theo expected her to leave in pursuit of these culinary delights, but she went on to say, brightly: 'Neither do I. Well – not the sorts of things most people eat, anyway.'

That explained the blood. 'Your table manners are not doing you much credit,' he said, keeping his back turned to her.

Her tone became sheepish; he pictured a blush. 'Yes, I have disgraced myself rather, have I not? Only I was too hungry to recollect much etiquette.' She went on to muse, not very amusingly, on the question of *due etiquette* when one supped from the veins of one's fellow man, rather than from a plate with proper use of a knife and fork; he was not listening, not until the word *ogre* penetrated the fog of his thoughts.

'An ogre?' He turned then, swiftly, and stared at the lady. 'Do you mean to tell me you attacked an *ogre* for a meal?'

'Come now, *attack* is an unpleasant word, is not it?' She smiled hopefully. 'I was not trying to *kill* him, I assure you. Nor even to hurt him, more than a little bit.'

'I know of only one ogre,' Theo said shortly. 'And he would not like to be made a dinner of for an impolite young chit.' This thought, too, penetrated his consciousness slowly; when it did, he began to laugh.

The irritating young lady observed this alteration with palpable relief. 'Do you know, I was beginning to feel you were angry with me?' she confided.

'Merely thought you a fool,' said Theo, still chuckling. 'Still do, as a matter of fact. Do you not know that your dinner is a Bow Street Runner?'

'He did mention something of that sort,' she admitted. 'You are acquainted with him? But you do not look as though you can have any recent acquaintance, sir. You are stepped out of a painting, I am sure of it.'

Theo remembered his outlandish attire. In the midst of his musical fugue he had, for a little while, forgotten it.

He remembered it now, with alacrity. He was not Lord Bedgberry in this moment; he was...whoever he wanted to be.

He gazed upon the smiling, bloodied face of his visitor in momentary panic. He was having wild thoughts of furthering his acquaintance with her – and had he not, only moments before, been finding her an aggravation?

But a few moments before, he had been himself; now he was somebody else.

'Your thirst appears to be slaked, ma'am, but mine is not,' he said. 'Shall you assist me in identifying a suitable meal?'

'I should be delighted,' she beamed. 'For myself I have always found it wisest to choose a stout, hearty sort. Prominent veins, and a good flow. What is your own opinion?'

'I have supped mostly on rabbits,' said Theo – and Theo he was again, depressingly, for a moment. 'But tonight I shall dine like a king,' he continued, shaking his old self off again, like a worn-out coat. 'And I shall follow your advice, Miss...?'

'Jendring,' she supplied, and stopped in order to make him a curtsey. 'Antonia Jendring.'

Theo bowed, in his courtliest manner. 'I am Lord Bedgberry,' he said.

'Yes, I should think you would be hungry,' she said, puzzlingly. 'A lifetime of rabbits, and scarcely a taste of the finest viands! How sorry an existence.'

So he was not to supply this shining young person with his identity, was he? So much the better. He had never before felt shamed by his dining habits, but he was beginning to be so. Why should not he help himself to the best? He had never killed anyone, nor would he do so now. A man may live just as well with a little less blood in his veins.

A worrisome thought occurred to him.

'You left Ballantine in acceptable health, I trust?'

'If you refer to my ogre, then yes. He left the room on his own two legs, I assure you.'

'In a fine temper, too, I should imagine,' said Theo.

'No, in fact he took it rather well.' They were following the hubbub of voices and laughter, inexorably approaching the dining-room. There was a light in her clear eyes, and a spring in her step; perhaps she was not entirely without inclination for dessert.

'If anybody may get away with a savage attack upon a Runner, I imagine it would be a fair lady like yourself.' Theo, unused to turning a pretty compliment, stumbled a little over the sentiment, but it was accepted: the lady laughed prettily.

'He did not strike me as susceptible to just any lady's smiles,' she remarked.

The conversation dropped, for they were arrived at the dining-room: beyond the door, uproar.

The chamber was fully the size of two handsome ballrooms, and crowded with long, wide tables spread with crimson brocade. The quantity of dishes dazzled the eyes: roast beef and pork and lamb glistening with gravy; great, heaped platters of pies and pastry tarts; jellies both savoury and sweet, wrought in a plethora of fanciful shapes; steaming tureens of copper, or silver, or gold, bearing a medley of soups; salads and roasted vegetables served in enormous bowls; a vast cake on every table, several layers tall and slathered in sweet icing. And *fruit*, towering pyramids of it, white pears and green apples – peaches, nectarines, pineapples even – jugs of clear water and punch – decanters of wine – Theo stared.

He had rarely had occasion to regret the specific (and limited) nature of his own sustenance, but today he did. For the guests of the masquerade were most happily employed in feasting, though the hour was not far short of three in the morning. Every plate bore a mound of delectable things; every glass brimmed with beverages. If he had criticised Miss Jendring's manners, well, those of her fellow guests were little better. They were gorging themselves on provender, every one of them.

'Curious,' Theo mused.

'Yes, is not it?' Miss Jendring agreed. 'I had thought to expect polite society.'

'I prefer this.' Theo regarded the chaos with a strange sense of approval: how far removed this merry repast from the staid, starched parades of refinement these gentlemen and ladies customarily enjoyed! If enjoyed was the proper term. No one had ever found a dinner party very diverting, Theo was certain of it.

'I can see why!' answered his companion, gaily. 'So entertained are they, who will notice a bite or two about the neck? Or care for it, if they did? You may choose at your leisure, I am sure.'

Theo adjusted his ideas. The tables held a mesmerising banquet for the diners; the chairs held an unprecedented feast for him.

The thought produced a smile.

But before he had taken more than a single step, an unwelcome sight arrested him where he stood: Gussie, sitting beside Lord Maundevyle, both of them deep in platters of confectionery. Gussie's eyes, though, were fixed squarely upon him: she was half-frowning, that odd expression she developed when she had got hold of an idea.

Had she somehow recognised him?

She had; surely she had. She was getting up, bidding Henry (with a careless word) to wait (which he did); coming his way.

She curtseyed.

'Miss Jendring,' she said. 'Do introduce me to your companion.'

'You are acquainted with Miss Jendring?' he said, in surprise – belatedly understanding that it was not *he* upon whom she had focused her attention, but on the lady beside him.

'We are recently introduced.' Gussie smiled perfunctorily. 'Have you deciphered the identity of your mysterious companion yet? I cannot permit you to outshine me in the Dance, you know.'

'Oh, are you then competing? I shall not get in your way.' Miss Jendring beamed. 'The gentleman and I were comparing our different experiences as to dining. He has quite shocked me. Subsisting upon rabbits! Only imagine.'

If she had hoped to shock Miss Werth, she was (of course) disappointed. 'Oh, you are Theo,' said Gussie, in tones of the bitterest disappointment.

Theo felt the same, as the mirage that transformed his character shattered, and fell away. 'Yes,' he sighed. 'It seems that I am.'

Gussie, perceiving some little part of his dismay, patted his arm. 'Never mind, cousin. You were among the last hold-outs, you know. I believe there is only that odd queen of a woman left in mummery, now.'

'I have observed her,' volunteered Miss Jendring, unexpectedly. 'I wonder if anyone shall decipher her identity?'

'I should hope so, for I have reason to believe—' Gussie, abruptly, stopped, and eyed Miss Jendring sideways.

'Reason to believe – what?' prompted Theo.

Gussie lifted her chin. 'She has done something that has displeased me excessively. The more so because she has done it while anonymous, thus balking me of my well-deserved victory over Mr. Ballantine.'

Theo found it impossible to comprehend this muddled speech, and said so, causing Gussie to sigh.

'Mr. Ballantine?' echoed Miss Jendring. 'That nice ogre?'

'*Nice* ogre? Nice?' Gussie blinked, incredulous. 'That settles it. This truly is the strangest place I have ever been to.' The thought brightened her spirits, for she smiled again, and straightened her shoulders. 'It is marvellous,' she pronounced, and returned to her dinner.

Theo regarded his companion rather sadly.

'So you are called Theo,' she said, probingly.

'Lord Bedgberry, more rightly.' He sighed – there was no use trying to hide it – and went on. 'Theodore Werth, that is. Miss Werth is my cousin.'

'And Lord Werth, the corpse-reviver, is your father! Delightful! I have been longing to meet you.' Theo found himself presented with a slender hand to shake; he did so.

'You are a puzzling young lady,' he said, wonderingly.

'Mama has often said so,' answered she, serene. 'Did you still want to eat?'

Theo regarded the diners once more. Strange, how differently the same scene now struck him: the merriment turned to vulgarity, the noise become discordancy, the diners' relish no longer endearing but rather unseemly. How great a difference a frame of mind makes, thought he, with no more idea how to alter it.

Had he enjoyed, for so brief a period, being a person of bon-homie, of expansive humour, of flirtatious charm? He had.

Would he have continued to enjoy it, had he been able to maintain the pretence for very much longer?

A little soul-searching, there: the answer came slowly.

No.

The thought cheered him. 'I do,' he replied. 'But I believe I will enquire of the kitchens.'

APRIL 30TH

Poor Theo. With all the advantages of glamorous Mummery to entertain him, and yet, to be so easily seen through! What can he mean by talking to Miss Jendring of rabbits, when he might have talked to her of any other subject in the world? How like him. Mind you, I observed a great quantity of spilled blood marring that lady's neck and gown; I venture to hope that her gentle charms might have lured him away from the blood of herbivores, and tempted him to sample better game. If so, I will take my hat off to the enterprising Antonia (for enterprising I do believe her to be: she has set her cap at Theo, I make no doubt. As a sister-in-law I believe I would prefer her to Clarissa, however, so I shall hold my peace on the subject).

Speaking of Clarissa: the most maddening thing! Fully an hour did I spend with her brother at my elbow, searching high and low for the fiendish disguise I had no doubt she would be hiding under. And then! To encounter her at dinner! Up to her eyebrows in Dutch cream pudding and flummery, absolutely herself in face and feature, and revoltingly composed! She was exploring, she informed me, and ignored the Mummer's Dance entirely. I have not yet forgiven her.

I grow weary at last, I confess, for we have spent most of the night in high revelry. Many of us, anyway. I have not seen my aunt or uncle in some hours; perhaps they retired to bed. If so, they missed dinner, and what a dinner it was! If this is to be the pattern of our days here – they are to be nights, rather, entertainments beginning at midnight, and dinner served much later – I shall be well pleased. I never saw so much of the night-hours before.

I have not seen Mr. Ballantine since before dinner, either, and as such have not had any opportunity to tell him of the infuriating woman with the Tudor garb and the aggravating attitude. Not to mention the loss of my pearls. I have not yet decided how I shall tell him. It is lowering; instead of discovering a thief, I have become a victim of robbery myself. Perhaps I will not tell him, at least until I have apprehended the culprit. That would set all to rights, would not it?

Gussie sat at the desk in her own chamber, wrapped in a thick shawl, and with a cup of wine (nearly empty) before her. She had returned to find Frosty fast asleep in an armchair in Gussie's own room, and had not disturbed her, save to cover her with a blanket: the night was cold indeed, high up in the mountains as they were. Great-Uncle Silvester dozed atop the mantelpiece, resembling a repellent statue, still as death, and as silent. Frosty, she thought, may well have chosen to remain above-stairs, rather than join in the games; she would find so large and noisy a gathering trying for her nerves. Silvester, though... he had disappeared the moment the carriage had deposited the family at the gates of the palace, and she could no more guess where he had been since than she could fly.

She set down her pen, and drifted to the long window. Little could be determined beyond the frosted glass, for the dawn had yet to break, and the night was dark, depthless shadow. Only a sliver of moon, waning to nothing, cast a wan glow over the distant peaks, and lent a faint shimmer to the air.

A magical place. A dangerous place. And still, no sign of the Lord and Lady.

Gussie had never learned the identity of the enigmatic woman who had (most probably) absconded with her pearls. She had never seen the woman again, in fact. Most likely, someone else had encountered her, and identified her, and – for all Gussie knew – the same woman had been her neighbour at dinner, her own face restored. How was she to catch such a person, when she possessed not a single clue as to their identity? She could not even say, with any certainty, that the thief was a woman: her semblance had been, but then Gussie's own disguise had made of her a man for the evening. There may have been a man behind the handsome lady's guise, too.

These were no satisfactory reflections to take with her into slumber. She sighed, turned away from the window, and returned to Frosty's side. Her companion had scarcely stirred. It was not good for her to sleep upright, in so awkward a posture, and she was no young woman to easily recover from the aches and pains of a morning. But so deep in sleep was she, Gussie had not the heart to wake her. She retired, then, to her own bed, and fell at once into an exhausted, and not very restful, slumber, in which dreams of the taunting, velvet-gowned queen alternated with visions of the peculiar Miss Jendring, bloodied with gore, and smiling like an angel as she tore out Theo's throat.

Somewhere in her sleep, Gussie smiled.

DAY 2:
MISRULE

CHAPTER TWELVE

GUSSIE WOKE TO AN afternoon bathed in a cool, silverish sunlight. The day was all but gone, she judged, the sun already on the point of setting into the horizon. Someone had come in while she slept, for a fire blazed in the hearth, and a basin of steaming water stood waiting atop the wash-stand. Gussie availed herself of this at once, grateful for the warmth of the water on her face and neck. She was unused to liquor, and uncertain whether so much of it agreed with her. Parts of her anatomy emphatically felt that it did *not* — most notably, her head.

Nothing that a hearty breakfast could not mend.

Gussie was halfway to her dressing-room before it occurred to her that the rumpled nest of blankets in her armchair still contained Miss Frostell, too.

'Frosty, have not you slept enough yet? Come, you must get up. Your poor limbs will ache dreadfully.'

Miss Frostell did not stir. Frowning, Gussie crossed the room and bent over her former governess, and gently shook the blanket. 'Frosty?'

The realisation was slow in dawning: no movement whatsoever met her eye, not even the slight rise-and-fall of inhalation and exhalation. Miss Frostell was not breathing.

Gussie's own breath stopped. 'Frosty.' She touched Miss Frostell's face, gently, then shook her, quite hard. 'Frosty, this is not—come now, no funning, so cruel a joke must be Clarissa's province, not yours. Frosty?'

Great-Uncle Silvester woke with a start, and uttered so harsh a laugh as to make Gussie jump. He launched himself from the mantelpiece in a flurry of beating wings, spraying gouts of stone-dust into the air, and landed awkwardly on Miss Frostell's head. 'Died in the night,' he said, with unwonted clarity.

'No.' Gussie shook her head, a feeling of wild panic overtaking her senses. 'She hasn't. She cannot have. Silvester, make her wake. Please.'

Great-Uncle Silvester merely cackled, a horrible sound devoid of mirth.

'Fetch my uncle,' she pleaded with him. 'Fetch Lord Werth. He will mend this.' It would not be a return to true life for Frosty, not as she had been. Gussie's heart twisted at the prospect, for while *she* could have no objection to Miss Frostell as revenant, she feared that Frosty would deplore it.

But to leave her in death; to lose her! No.

Some part of these thoughts steadied her: she calmed, and bent to a clearer-headed examination of the scene. What could have caused Frosty to expire like this? She had been in excellent health the night before, and while she was no longer young, she was not so very old, either.

An awful thought occurred: Gussie pulled back the blanket, and examined Miss Frostell's corpse more thoroughly. She was cool to the touch, so she had been dead some hours; had she been dead already when Gussie had come in, and gone to bed? Perhaps. But no alarming sight met her searching gaze: no knives buried hilt-deep in poor Frosty's flesh, no bruises to her throat, no blue-tinged features and bulging eyes. No signs, then, of murder, by weapon or smothering or any other method: Miss Frostell looked as though she had drifted off to sleep, and stayed there.

Not that anybody could have any possible reason to murder Frosty. A more inoffensive person Gussie could scarcely imagine: everyone loved her. She had even charmed the repulsive (or formerly repulsive) Charles Selwyn.

Gussie had completed this unhappy investigation and returned to the window before her uncles arrived, one flapping his frenzied way over the threshold only to collide with the wall (a sickening crunch alerting Gussie to the mishap; she turned to witness Silvester crash into the carpet, in a puff of dust). The other entered at a more sedate pace, but quick enough. Lord Werth took in the scene with a calm eye, uttered the syllable 'Ah', and was by Frosty's side in an instant.

'I do not know what can have happened,' Gussie explained, keeping out of her uncle's way: let him work, the sooner then poor Frosty would be revived. 'She was asleep in this chair when I retired to bed – or so I thought, it never entered my head that I ought to check for a heartbeat. When I woke just now, I could not rouse her.'

Lord Werth, attired still in a handsome patterned dressing-gown, merely nodded. He was touching Miss Frostell's hair, her cheek, her forehead, his gestures similar to Gussie's own, when she had (still unwitting) been attempting to wake her companion. His, though, held all the eldritch power of the Wyrde, and wake she would: wake she *must*, for Lord Werth called to the very bones of her.

Only, she did not.

'Uncle?' said Gussie, after a few minutes had passed, and Miss Frostell remained silent, and inert.

Lord Werth straightened, and beheld the lifeless corpse with a frown. His hands went into the pockets of his dressing-gown, his thoughts went – nowhere Gussie could follow.

At length he said: 'She will not rouse.'

Gussie had no answer in her. Frosty would not rouse? Impossible. Unthinkable.

'This has… has such a thing ever happened before, Uncle?' she ventured at last.

'No.'

Silence, then; both stood still, appalled. Miss Frostell would not rouse. Lord Werth had no power to make her.

Frosty was gone.

Gussie felt like a child, small and diminished. Not that loss was unknown to her; her own parents were long departed, and both had declined to return in a state of undeath. Her sister Nell spoke to them still, when she visited the Towers – their shades, at least. To Gussie, they were simply gone.

But this loss had occurred when she was but a small child. She barely remembered her mother and father, and Lord and Lady Werth had well supplied their place in her life.

Miss Frostell was different. Frosty had been as much a mother to her as Lady Werth – in some ways, more so. Frosty had been her comfort, her support, her ally in everything. Frosty was as much a fixture in her life as the Wyrde, as immoveable as the earth itself. Whenever she died, Gussie had known – *known* – that Lord Werth would return her to semblance, at least, of life and limb; she would never truly be gone.

But she was.

'Well,' she said at last, the word a sigh. 'Frosty packed mourning gowns. I taxed her with it, of course. What use am I like to have for mourning blacks, said I, on a mere few days' house party? "Better to be prepared, my dear," she said, and she is proved right again.' Gussie spoke, as far as she was able, with her customary pragmatism, but a tremor here and there gave her away.

Her uncle regarded her with silent sympathy, and laid a hand on her shoulder. 'I will send Goodspeed to you. And Mr. Ballantine.'

Gussie glanced at him, sharp. 'Mr. Ballantine? You think, then, that something untoward has happened here.'

'I do not think that,' he said gently. 'There are no signs of it. But it is strange, for all that, and it had better be looked into.'

Gussie would not oppose such a decision. She sat instead on the broad arm of Frosty's chair, and took the poor, thin, dead hand in her own. How slender the fingers. Frosty had always had an air of frailty to her, though Gussie had known few people with greater strength or energy.

She was engaged in staring sightlessly at the carpet, stroking Frosty's hand clutched still in her own, when a furious pounding began on her door.

She was up in an instant, across the room, and throwing it open. 'What now?'

Clarissa had dressed in a hurry: her blue gown fitted oddly, and she had a mismatched shawl in a lurid red paisley over her shoulders. Her hair... better not say too much about the state of her hair. 'Henry is dead and Mama is beside herself and I cannot find your uncle—Ah! I had hoped you might find him, Gussie, but here he is. Lord Werth, I beg and beseech you, revive poor Henry. I believe Mama will give you all our worldly goods if you want them, if you will only restore him to us.'

'Lord Maundevyle? Dead.' Gussie turned the thought over in her mind, finding it – odd. A curious fact, prompting little feeling in her. Perhaps she was so shocked at Frosty's demise as to feel numbed, unable to take in any further tragedy.

Or perhaps the stirring of unease in her gut told a different story.

'What are the chances?' she asked of her uncle.

He came to stand beside her, frowning. 'Infinitesimal, I would say.'

Clarissa grew impatient. 'Come, come, will you help us? I hate to *rush* you, my lord, but—'

'Frosty is dead,' Gussie interrupted. 'Look.' She stepped aside, out of Clarissa's way: behind her stood the armchair, and Miss Frostell's corpse.

Clarissa stared, thunderstruck.

'So your brother is not the only unexplained corpse we have on our hands this morning,' Gussie continued. Her spirits were rising with every word. 'Unless,' she added, struck again by a dark thought, 'unless the mode of his death is—Clarissa, he has not been *murdered*, has he?'

An impatient shake of the head gave her answer. 'How should I know? I do not believe he has, there are no bloodied weapons sticking out of him, or anything obvious like that. He looks like your poor Frosty, there. Asleep, only not.' She was harried; the rush of words tumbled out, barely comprehensible. Gussie wondered if her brother had understood that she cared about him.

'There is something strange going on,' Gussie declared, heartened. 'Depend upon it, they are not dead at all! It is something else.'

'He does seem very dead, Gussie,' Clarissa disagreed. She crossed to Miss Frostell's chair, and inspected the corpse there. 'So does Frosty, you must allow. Oh, I forgot.' She approached Gussie, next, and bestowed upon her an awkward embrace. 'My commiserations.'

'And mine,' Gussie retorted, perfunctorily. 'Now get off me. We have work to do.'

THEO HAD NEVER TROUBLED himself to seek his bed. Overfed – on blood, and chocolate, and wine — he had retired, in a manner of speaking, to a chaise longue in an alcove, not far from the dining room. Weariness and inebriation had sunk him into slumber at last, halfway through a chapter on proper embalming procedure, and he woke with the musty scent of old paper in his nostrils: the book had dropped onto his face, and remained there while he slept.

Several other recumbent forms lay here and thereabout, relieving Theo of his transitory embarrassment. He had not been the only gentleman to over indulge to an unaccustomed degree, then. He even saw one or two ladies, felled like wilted blossoms, their silken gowns crumpled about their skewed limbs like crushed petals.

What a shocking display of hedonism. And it was only the first day.

Theo ignored those he passed, for his head hurt, and every step sent a fresh stab of pain through his temples. He staggered on, unconscious of any direction or particular goal – until halted by a glimpse of a familiar ice-blue gown.

'Miss Jendring?' He stopped, and tried not to stare, but how could he help it; the woman made such a spectacle – *more* bloodied even than before, what an appetite she had. She had not even reposed herself upon a divan, or a chair, or anything so civilised. Instead she lay slumped in a corner, one shoe missing, her hair askew and her eyes deeply shadowed.

Theo, prickling with discomfort, briefly considered fleeing the scene. But no. That would not do. They had shared confidences, the previous evening, even if most of that had occurred while Theo was under a disguise. That made her a friend – of sorts. And one did not abandon a friend in need, not unless there was some particular advantage to be gained by it.

He knelt down, and tugged awkwardly on a loose fold of her gown. 'Miss Jendring. Ma'am? This is no proper place for you to be sleeping. I strongly advise a removal to a suitable bedchamber; no doubt you were assigned one. Miss Jendring?'

How deeply she slept.

No.

Theo felt cold horror wash over him, if only for an instant. She was dead, of course. He had known it for some moments, though his mind had insisted on denial of the clear facts. Her corpse-white face: dead. Her eyes, half open, and glassy: dead.

Her slackness of posture, limbs akimbo: dead. Her eery stillness, no rise and fall to her blood-stained torso: dead.

The blood.

He leaned nearer, attempting, with his bleary and aching eyes, to determine the nature of the blood stains. Were they merely the vestiges of a hearty repast, or had she been stabbed, or something equally horrible?

He detected no wounds on her, no sign of bodily trauma whatsoever. She had merely sat down here, and – died.

How curious.

Theo sat back on his heels, thinking. People did not ordinarily just — expire like this, did they? Not *young* people, at any rate. One might feel little surprise if one's elderly grandmama were discovered cold and stone-dead in her armchair of a morning, but a fresh young lady like Miss Jendring?

Yet, she did not seem to have been killed, as far as he could detect. She might, of course, have been poisoned...

He leapt to his feet, arrested by the sudden recollection of just how many inelegantly reposing forms he had wandered past only moments before. Were they sleeping, or had *everybody* died in their sleep, save Theo alone?

'At least I would get some peace and *quiet*, then,' he muttered, but curiosity had hold of him, and would not release him to the period of repose his aching head so sorely needed. *Had* every-body died in the night? How intriguing, if so! He investigated.

Ten minutes' work swiftly established clear facts. Of the bod-ies littered thereabouts, he discovered four to be yet living – and indignant, for some reason, at being poked and prodded, just as though they had not left their unconscious bodies lying about for anybody to develop ideas about.

Two were dead. Dead as doornails, dead as felled trees, dead as Great-Uncle Silvester. 'That doesn't seem normal,' he observed.

'It isn't.'

He jumped. Clarissa! How had she crept up on him? He whirled about, and directed at her a quelling frown.

She ignored this, as usual. 'Are they all dead?' she asked, with lively curiosity. She was dressed like a footwoman again, a sight to which he was growing accustomed.

'Only three of them.'

'Only three! Not as bad as I feared.'

'Why?'

Clarissa smiled her savage smile, just at him. 'I discovered my beloved brother Henry's lifeless remains not an hour ago. Your cousin is similarly engaged with the corpse of your charming Miss Frostell. I have not told Charles yet. He is doing so well of late. It would be a pity to ruin it already.'

Theo absorbed this news in stoic silence.

'You do not seem much dismayed,' Clarissa observed.

'Well, I'm not.'

'Some might consider that cold-hearted.'

Theo shrugged up his shoulders. 'They are dead and gone: what is the use of repining? No quantity of tears will bring them back.'

'Do not you think it strange, that so many guests should die in the night – apparently, of nothing?'

'Perhaps they were all poisoned, at that absurd feast.' But even as he spoke, he remembered Miss Jendring. She was like him: she did not eat the food that sustained regular creatures. She had, in all probability, imbibed nothing of the over-plentiful banquet. Yet, she too lay dead.

'I ate like a pig,' Clarissa informed him. 'Like a whole herd of pigs, in fact. I made a point of tasting every single dish, and yet here I stand, alive.'

'More's the pity.'

The grin returned, more savage than ever. 'Yes, isn't it? One point of detail that might interest you, however: your uncle has tested his Wyrde on Miss Frostell, and found himself helpless. He has tried Henry, too. He can do nothing.'

'You have some theory, perhaps, as to why this is.'

'As a matter of fact, I do.'

Theo waited.

'Are you going to tell me what it is?' he prompted, when she did not speak.

'How kind of you to ask. My theory is: they are not dead. At least, not in any regular way.'

Theo stared at the nearest corpse, a portly man in his fifties at least, his eyes wide open, and staring sightlessly at nothing. 'Forgive me, Miss Selwyn, but I have scarcely beheld a deader deadman than that man is right now.'

'Coming from a Werth, that is a declaration that must hold considerable weight,' she replied, solemnly. 'Nonetheless.'

'Nonetheless, you prefer to cling to an outlandish hypothesis, with not a scrap of evidence to support it.'

'Perhaps I prefer to hope that my brother is not gone forever.'

'That is sentiment.'

Clarissa gazed at him with an odd expression in her sardonic eyes. 'You have no use for sentiment, I see.'

'It has never got anybody very far, that I can tell.'

'That depends entirely on where one is hoping to go.'

Theo had no answer to that, never having wanted to go anywhere that sentiment might take him. 'I suppose we had better bury them,' he suggested, in place of a reply.

'No indeed. Your cousin and I are determined to revive them all, every one.'

'I might have known Gussie would have something to do with so mad an idea.'

'Yes, is not she marvellous?'

Theo judged it best to abstain from responding to so absurd a remark. 'What then do you suggest we do with them?'

'We cannot leave them where they are? They are not so very in the way.' She cast a critical glance about the hallway, replete as it was with alcoves and sprawled bodies, and wrinkled her delicate nose. 'No, I see that we cannot. Hm. There are attics, I suppose: let them be conveyed up there.'

'I have no intention of spending my morning hauling dead persons up flights of stairs,' Theo informed her severely, ruining the effect rather by adding, 'My head hurts too much.'

'Mine, too,' Clarissa agreed. 'The footmen may be employed, I daresay.'

Theo had not caught so much as a glimpse of the liveried footpersons that whole morning, but did not choose to debate the point with Clarissa. Let her deal with the suitable disposal of the bodies, if she would.

'I wonder what the festivities are to be today?' he mused aloud.

'How very Wyrde of you.'

'I do not understand that remark.'

'Surrounded by the decaying remains of the young and beautiful, and you are thinking only of parties. A Werth trait, is it?'

Theo looked again at the stout gentleman nearby, felled with his embroidered waistcoat half unbuttoned over his swelling paunch.

'I was wondering,' he muttered, 'whether this mass departure from the mortal coil might have something to do with it.'

'Ah! So you agree, they are not dead.'

'I merely admit the possibility of some other, stranger explanation.'

Clarissa could be dazzling, when she was happy: she displayed some of this sparkling vivacity now, by way of a glittering smile. 'I *love* stranger explanations,' she declared, and danced away, bent upon who knew what nefarious mission.

Theo was left in solitary contemplation of the impromptu graveyard surrounding him. At least, he thought, they were not yet beginning to smell.

April 30th

Night has fallen, and has brought no enlightenment with it. The bodies have been removed to their bedchambers, and laid out upon the beds so recently assigned to them. Forty-three, in total, and among them are Henry, Miss Jendring, and – appallingly – my beloved Frosty.

The rest of my family persist in tolerable health, though my aunt remains largely absent from the proceedings. Considering the events of last night, I must consider her wise.

Goodspeed has taken charge of the corpses. Rarely have I been so grateful for his presence, for Lady Maundevyle is greatly discomposed by the deathly inertia of her son, and felt it necessary to be sure that we all knew it. One might expect her second son, Charles, to celebrate Lord Maundevyle's death, since he is his brother's heir (and a rather revolting person). However, he seems curiously stricken, as much by poor Frosty's apparent demise as by Henry's.

I have taken it upon myself to raise everyone's spirits by starting a much happier idea: this is some macabre game the Lord and Lady are playing upon us, and come the end of the masquerade all shall be revealed. I cannot, at present, imagine what the purpose of such a charade could be, but Clarissa has joined me in promoting the notion, and I am happy to report that the results are palpable. The guests were, collectively, rather depressed this afternoon; now, as the revelry is about to begin, there is an atmosphere of merriment once more, and anticipation. We are all agog to discover what fresh devilry is afoot.

For my own part, I—

Gussie's pen dropped from her hand, her journal entry incomplete, for of a sudden she found herself *elsewhere*. Tucked up in her own room, a moment before, and writing busily at her desk, she discovered herself to be transported, instantly and by unknown means, into somewhere else entirely.

Somewhere undesirably cold; she shivered. Her garments did not seem to be equal to the pervasive chill, and there was no fire in the hearth – in fact, there was no hearth at all. She stood in something of an attic garret, a cramped, rude chamber, furnished only with a narrow, comfortless bed and a wash-stand of no remarkable feature.

Her clothing had altered itself, too, just as on the previous night, when she had unconsciously donned the semblance of a nobleman out of history. Nothing so sumptuous for her tonight, however: she wore a drab, dark gown of some coarse stuff, the hem shorter than she customarily liked, and she felt the flimsy embrace of a cap of some sort over her hair.

Gussie detested caps. She shook the thing off, and discarded it; then, strode to the door, and hurled it open.

She was in the attic, she judged, for a narrow passage lay beyond. Several others were emerging from adjacent doors, all garbed as she was, plainly – except for one young gentleman, who had acquired the black-and-silver garb of a footman.

With a start, she recognised the features of one of her neighbours at dinner, the night before.

'Mr. Portman?'

The man blinked stupidly at her. 'Miss Werth? How oddly you are dressed.'

'I might say the same of you.'

He glanced down at himself, and then again, a longer look. 'I am to be a footman tonight, I perceive.'

'And I, a maid.' Gussie shook out her coarse skirts, a gesture which summarily failed to make a handsome gown of them. 'I preferred last night's illusion, I admit.'

'We are not to serve at dinner, are we?' Mr. Portman, aghast at the idea, looked wildly about, as though there might be somewhere to run from so hideous a prospect.

Gussie smiled. 'I wonder if our servants feel the same way, every other night of the year?' She paused in brief thought, and added, 'I wonder *whom* we are to serve at dinner, if we are most of us become servants for the night? For I make no doubt, a great quantity of us are up here, turned into footmen and maids. The rest of us are likely down in the kitchens, and what a terrible prospect *that* is, for there shall not be a scrap of food prepared that could be worth the eating.'

Mr. Portman had no chance to respond, for the distant tones of that ghastly organ started up again, and drowned out the last few words of Gussie's sentence. If only someone had slain the organist! Forty-three fresh corpses, and the organ-player could not have been among them? How cruel a mistress was Fate.

The Mummer's Dance had begun upon the playing of the organ. Gussie supposed this fresh bout of orchestral hysterics heralded the beginning of the second day's entertainments, though she was no nearer to understanding their nature than she had been before. Someone thought it amusing to make servants of the gentry; doubtless also, to make gentry of the servants.

A neat little piece of irony, that. Gussie could almost appreciate it, if someone's idea of wit had not condemned her to an evening of hard labour.

Though: had it? Her gentlemen's garb had been but a costume: perhaps this was, too.

'Oh, Gussie. How well you look.' Lady Werth, arrayed similarly to her niece, appeared from the midst of the growing crowd of confused and displaced gentry milling about above-stairs. Lord Werth attended her, his wife's hand on his arm, just as though they were en route to an evening party, or a ball: he, garbed in the spruce black garments of a butler, or possibly a valet, had lost nothing of his customary dignity.

'Do I, Aunt? How odd of you to say so.'

'It is not clothes that determine a woman's style, but attitude. You, my dear, look ready to slay an army.'

Gussie waved this off. 'So I always am, but I am rarely applauded for it. You have heard about Frosty, have you?'

Lady Werth's face clouded. 'I am very sorry for it.'

'Precisely. She must be retrieved from wherever she has gone, as must all the others – I am by no means prepared to relinquish Lord Maundevyle either – and, therefore, one must be prepared to encounter any difficulty.'

'And if they are, indeed, dead, my dear?'

'They are not. I will answer for it that they are not.'

Lady Werth wisely forbore to pursue the argument – too accustomed, in all probability, to losing them. 'Shall we descend?' she murmured, herself the picture of serenity, not a trace of incipient frost to be seen anywhere about her person.

A gong sounded, resonant and echoing. Then another, and another. 'Dinner is early today,' Gussie remarked, and followed in the train of those already streaming towards the stairs. 'Let us see what we are about.'

The descent from the attics was no speedy business, there being a large number of "servants" to filter down a large number of staircases – cramped and winding at first, then broadening into wider, handsomer stairs on the lower floors of the house. When, at last, they streamed from the last carpeted steps into an enormous hall, the chatter of excited, laughing voices echoing off the vaulted ceiling, Gussie felt unusually winded. Where her fellow guests were finding the spare breath to talk was beyond her.

'A real maid must be in far better health than I,' she gasped. 'Up and down such stairs all day long! I would not volunteer for it.'

The hall was emptying rapidly; guests were disappearing through various of the several doors leading off it. Gussie chose one to her left, and made for it; her aunt and uncle chose one to her right, and wandered away; she found herself forthwith returned to the massive feasting chamber, and beheld Lord and Lady Werth arriving at the same time, close at hand.

'All doors lead to the feast,' she mused. 'Interesting.' Mr. Portman being nowhere in sight, her neighbours at this new banquet proved to be a willowy lady of advanced years and repellent aspect, and one of the younger Jendrings, whose name Gussie could not remember. The latter sat with woebegone demeanour, wreathed in misery, tears glistening in her eyes.

'Antonia would have so enjoyed this feast,' she declaimed, tragically, to Gussie.

Gussie knew enough of Antonia's habits to suspect otherwise, but declined to comment as such. 'Never mind,' she said, patting the girl's hand. 'She will enjoy the next one.'

A look of lachrymose reproach was all the reply she was to expect, seemingly, and Gussie resolved upon paying Miss Jendring no further heed.

A deep, thrumming noise sounded, and sounded again: a pounding that shook the floor. The guests turned, Gussie with them, seeking the source of the noise: in the centre of the bustling chamber stood a tall man, far taller than any living man Gussie had ever beheld before. He towered over the company, clad in black, silver, and white, his hair a fall of dark locks tumbling over his shoulders. A black velvet domino and matching mask lent him an aura of mystery, and he glittered with dark jewels. In his left hand he carried a silver sceptre; in his right, a mighty black staff.

When he spoke, his words rolled about the room like thunder.

'Ladies and Gentlemen of the Wyrde! The Feast of Fools is upon us.'

The withered woman on Gussie's right leaned nearer, and, with a waft of foul-smelling breath, hissed, 'The Lord at last!'

'So it appears,' Gussie agreed. 'But what is the Feast of Fools supposed to be?'

'La! The young, they know nothing.'

'That may be true, but does not presently enlighten me.'

The woman tutted. 'It is an ancient custom. Topsy-turvy, we shall all be, until the Lord of Misrule declares the revelry over.'

Gussie had not ceased to watch the Lord, for he fascinated her: everything about him drew the eye, mesmerised.

'Oh, I doubt it is to be he,' said her neighbour, following the line of her gaze. 'The Feast of Fools is chaos entirely, child. Tonight's Master of Ceremonies will be selected at random.'

Gussie directed an enquiring gaze at her loquacious companion. 'How do you know all this, ma'am? I never heard of such a proceeding.'

'I am older than I look.' This enigmatic statement being followed with an unpleasantly fragrant laugh, Gussie recoiled. The woman looked a century old, at least, and smelled like the grave; she could be unfathomably ancient.

Gussie judged politeness sensible in the face of such antiquity, and proffered her thanks; her attention was soon, perforce, returned to the Lord of the Palace, for his sceptre had drifted from his hand, and now hung suspended high in the air. Silver glinted in the light of hundreds of candles as it turned slowly, far above their heads.

'Far be it from me to dictate!' the Lord was saying, in his booming baritone. 'The sceptre shall select for us the Master of Misrule. Keep very still in your chairs, children!'

As he spoke, the sceptre began to float this way and that, humming something fey and discordant as it spun. Once, it descended, almost into the waiting grasp of a gentleman in sumptuous green; he made a catch at it, missed, and swore in the uncouth vowels of a farmer. His neighbours laughed, as did the Lord, his laughter a deep cackle that chilled Gussie to her core. She shivered, most agreeably.

Twice more the sceptre taunted, hesitating over a sour-faced young lady in crimson silk, then a man in footman's livery, with a bristling moustache and a purple mark spread up the left side of his neck.

'Three measured, and found wanting!' announced the Lord. 'Who shall be next?'

Theo must be somewhere in the room, Gussie realised, as must Great-Aunt Honoria: everyone had been summoned, herded to the feast like a flock of sheep. 'Don't choose Theo,' she groaned. 'Or my poor, addled aunt. Only imagine the punishment.'

The sceptre chose neither. It descended at last, in a decisive *swoop*, and settled (with a certain sense of inevitability, on Gussie's part) in the hands of a handsome old man in a pristine dark blue coat, his grey locks superbly arranged, his cravat white as snow, and a jewelled pin catching the light: it was Goodspeed.

'Why, what a nobleman he makes,' she marvelled.

'Do you, then, know the Master?' asked the crone, still nameless.

'He is my butler.'

The crone laughed, wheezing. 'Not tonight. You must do his bidding, Miss, for he is the Master of Misrule.'

'Is that how it works?' Gussie mused. 'I shall be intrigued to discover what Goodspeed would have me do.'

A throne stood on a dais at the far end of the hall: wide enough to seat three side-by-side, the thing was wrought from the finest mahogany, with golden fittings and cushions of indigo silk. Goodspeed, sceptre in hand and smiling, ascended the dais, and reposed himself upon it. Everything proclaimed him a king in both name and nature: appearance, posture, sumptuary.

'I do believe he is wasted as a butler,' Gussie added, with a small sigh.

Goodspeed smiled upon his subjects, as regal as he was congenial. Something in the very benignity of his manner gave Gussie a prickling of unease.

He stood, and as he did so his garb shimmered and changed: a Fool's motley it became, yet still a king's raiment, his cape ermine and blue velvet, his shoes jewelled with diamonds as well as bells. The jester's cap atop his grey head was a sumptuous black article, gilded and shining.

'I see ladies become maids, and footmen become lords!' he called. Something amplified his voice, sent it shattering over the hubbub of chatter: the guests quieted. 'Yet I feel we are not yet topsy-turvy enough. Let that be changed.' He waved his silver sceptre; it caught the light in so odd a way as to dazzle Gussie's eyes, and for a moment she could not see.

When her vision cleared, she beheld: darkness.

'Curious,' she said, flatly, not yet at all entertained. She was hungry, and some freak of Goodspeed's had got in between her and her dinner.

She moved forward, and stopped: her face had encountered a solid surface, perhaps a wall. Or a door... the obstruction vanished as she formed the thought, and she passed on, and into a dimly-lit bedchamber.

It was not her own. Whoever it belonged to had not used it at all, for the embroidered coverlets over the bed looked untouched. A quantity of peculiar articles adorned every surface: pots of white hair-powder atop the dressing-table, with a great deal of the stuff spread about like snow. Discarded gowns of last century's fashions, and hair ornaments to match. Spiders, crawling everywhere she looked.

'Great-Aunt Honoria?' Gussie called. She could not think why Goodspeed had resolved upon sending her into her aunt's bedchamber, especially when Honoria did not appear to be in residence.

She wafted about a little, seeking some clue to elucidate so odd an event. Nothing enlightened her; nothing, that is, until she passed out of the bedchamber and into an adjacent dressing-room, and there on the wall hung a mighty looking-glass in a golden frame. A candle burned in a sconce beside it, illuminating Gussie and her reflection.

From this she recoiled with a cry of horror, for something was *gravely* amiss with her figure.

To be specific, it was missing. All of it. Only her face remained, and her hair, the latter a little disordered (no doubt from the unseemly haste with which she had torn off the hated cap, and thrown it away).

Her body, neatly severed at the neck, was somewhere Gussie wasn't. Traces of blood marred the place where her head had been (apparently) chopped off; as she watched, more of it appeared, and descended in a thin stream towards the carpet.

This calmed her at once. 'I see! I am become my aunt. And she, no doubt, is wandering about somewhere in a live body again, being me.'

She would enjoy the adventure greatly, no doubt, and put Gussie's borrowed flesh to excellent use.

As for Gussie herself: she concentrated, thinking empty thoughts, and beheld, with great satisfaction, her severed head slowly fading to mist, and vanishing away. No reflection remained in the mirror.

'So that is how it's done,' she whispered. 'Magnificent!'

No thief could long escape her with invisibility at her disposal. With a cackle of glee, Gussie swooped off, passing through walls and doors with the greatest of ease, and went in search of her mother's pearls.

CHAPTER THIRTEEN

LADY SLEEP HAD NOT favoured Mr. Ballantine with her blessed presence in far too many hours.

He had been obliged — or he had *felt* obliged, which amounted to much the same thing – to attend the many scenes of abrupt and inexplicable death that had stricken the palace after the Mummer's Dance. All forty-three of them. Beginning, of course, with poor Miss Frostell, attended by an unusually stricken Gussie, and much of the rest of their family. She had, by all appearances, died peacefully in her sleep; as had Lord Maundevyle, and all the rest of them.

And the eldest Miss Jendring. In the course of investigating her demise, he discovered her to have various siblings: her younger sisters wept copiously over her fragile remains, and nobody thought it odd that he never asked about the blood on her.

Forty-three separate scenes of unexpected death, and not a single clue at any one of them. It was enough to drive a Runner mad, and he felt increasingly unhinged as the night wore on, and then the day after it. What could possibly cause such mass expiration? The only possible cause of death (had they been murdered) must be poison, as there was not a mark on any of them. But how had it been administered, and specifically to these forty or so people? Had there been one single contaminated dish at dinner, of which only these forty-three had partaken? If so, how was he ever to learn which it was?

And why would anybody have enacted so deranged a scheme? For as a method of murder it was wildly indiscriminate. There could be no conceivable *reason* behind it. He must be dealing with a madman.

Or, as Gussie persisted in believing, the poor souls were nowhere near as dead as they appeared. There may be some slight evidence for such an idea, he was forced to admit: the strange circumstance of Lord Werth's hitherto unassailably reliable powers failing to operate upon these particular dead persons was suggestive of *something*. However. Dead they appeared, and until they manifested some other, less inert mode of being, dead he must believe them to be.

He explored the kitchens, and thoroughly, but to no avail. The servants there were too busy to talk much to him, or even to each other. Robed in black and silver, like the footmen (and women), they were harried, efficient, and uncommunicative. The notion that one of their dishes might have been laced with something deadly met with collective disgust: the very idea! He had to admit, the likelihood that any guest had managed to slip something into the salamagundy without being intercepted or observed by these frighteningly efficient staff bordered upon nil.

Of course, it might have been one of these nameless paragons of unsmiling competence manning the kitchens. Someone grown tired of serving food to ungrateful gentry, and determined upon revenge.

As a theory, it was weak.

He snatched a few hours of restless slumber in his own room, somewhere late in the afternoon. A single day of entertainments, and already forty people lay dead; he would have advised an immediate withdrawal from the palace, save that they were isolated in some mysterious location without a road in sight, and no means of procuring the floating carriages by which they had arrived. They were stuck, then, until the event concluded, and a chilling prospect that had become.

Who knew what fresh disasters were to unfold, on the second day? The advent of midnight found him weary and uneasy, though to observe his fellow guests he was the only person so afflicted. Even Gussie seemed in high spirits, if of the brittle sort, suggestive of a strong effort. She and Miss Selwyn had been industrious in putting about the idea of its all being part some sort of charade: he hoped, for everyone's sake, they may be proved correct. Were they not, the two young ladies may find themselves summarily lynched.

At length came the distant chimes, twelve of them – and someplace other went Ballantine, without warning, and all in a rush. He looked about him in confusion from the vantage point of a grand chair – more like a throne, the thing, so large it was, and majestic. A gentleman's study, perhaps, or some such place: a fire blazed in a hearth with an ornate mahogany surround; bookcases comfortably filled with neatly-bound volumes lined the walls; an escritoire sat below one window.

'Mr. Ballantine?' said somebody at his elbow: the wings of his chair were so large as to obscure his vision. He'd not seen her.

He sat forward a little, and beheld: Mrs. Hayton, Lady Werth's abigail. Only she did not look like a lady's maid now, her gown as handsome as any of her noble employer's, her greying hair intricately arranged and adorned with jewelled combs.

'Ma'am,' said he, rising from his chair, and performing a bow. 'Some manner of charade makes a lord of me, and you a lady.'

She laughed, and turned about in her beautiful gown (silk, and the colour of jade stones, with silver embroidery). 'I find this charade more to my taste than that of yesterday.'

'I believe I shall also, provided it does not end the same way.'

'You refer to the poor dead folk. Yes, how shocking. Poor Miss Frostell! She was so gentle a soul.'

She might have enjoyed an evening's sport as a fine lady, Miss Frostell. The thought saddened Ballantine, until he recollected her diffident nature: more likely she would have retired to her own room with a cup of tea, and amused herself with a book.

The dinner gong sounded, several times, and the relative peace shattered under the clamour of many pairs of feet passing the door.

'Shall we, ma'am?' Ballantine offered Mrs. Hayton his arm.

She took it with an affected little flourish, and simpered. 'Thank you, sir.'

His unease returned in full force one the Lord had made his declaration, and turned loose his sceptre; a random selection, not at all contrived! A likely story. And the Master of such ceremonies as these must have unusual arts at his or her disposal... Ballantine sat with his heart pounding while the sceptre dithered over its choice, half expecting some disastrous person to be given its charge (Clarissa, say, or even worse, Gussie).

Goodspeed, though. Goodspeed was sensible, capable, and unthreatening; Ballantine relaxed, had leisure to look about himself, to anticipate dinner.

Nothing of the sort being forthcoming, he had leisure – just – to grow uneasy again, *before*—

'*I feel we are not yet topsy-turvy enough. Let that be changed,*' declared the Master—

—Topsy turvy, and all turned change-about once more. Had he just lauded Goodspeed for his sense? And then to play such a trick—

—He felt different in some unspeakable way, no longer the sturdy, thief-taking figure to which he was accustomed, but taller (a little), his figure more slight, his strength palpably lessened.

A strange thirst in his throat, unfamiliar.

His fine, new, lordly garb changed again already, altered to a good cutaway coat in sober blue, an unpretentious waistcoat, no jewellery: nothing fussy.

The dining room had faded from his senses, taking its bustle and its noise with it. Now he stood in a dressing-room, so he judged from its meanness of proportion and the quantity of looking-glasses. Someone had been using it for something other than dressing, however, for several books lay scattered about, one or two left lying open, all with scraps of paper stuffed between the pages to hold the place. Untidy. Yet the garments were ordered and well maintained, neatness itself: somebody had a valet who knew his work, and also his place, and never touched his master's tomes.

A terrible suspicion dawned in Ballantine's mind.

With the hasty step of dawning horror, he approached one of the glasses, and stared.

He retained his own face and features: recognisable enough. But all else was altered. He was Hugh Ballantine, as he might have been had he been born the son of Lord and Lady Werth, brought up in ease and oddity, cerebral and bookish, and – strange. He was Theodore Werth, and he was *hungry*.

'Oh, Goodspeed,' he growled, backing away from the mirror. 'What I would not do to *you* in this moment...'

The real Theo was, doubtless, wandering the halls somewhere in the guise of an ogre, and what a bumbling scholar like that peculiar young man might not do with such brawn at his disposal – it was like to go to his head, as feeble as he was all the rest of his days. Ballantine flexed his thin-fingered hands, misliking the lack of strength to them.

'Don't you look a treat.'

Ballantine spun, searching the shadowed room to no effect: he saw no one. 'Gussie,' he called, and hauled open the nearest wardrobe. No impish young women hiding in there: the next, and the next he tore through, and found no one. 'Where are you, you maddening creature?'

A peal of laughter answered him. 'You will never guess.'

Ballantine thought quickly. If the mysterious powers of the Master of Misrule could mix *him* up with Theo, what unearthly horror might they have wrought upon Gussie?

'You had better not be a revenant, Miss Werth,' he thundered. 'Naught but a head, like your Great-Aunt Honoria! That is it, isn't it?'

The air shimmered a few feet away: Gussie's face appeared, smiling. 'Such insights I have into my aunt's habits! I quite understand her fascination with spying. It is the most diverting pastime.'

'And unconscionably rude!'

'Yes, that, of course.'

Ballantine glowered.

'What if one were to be putting one's unconscionably rude powers to excellent use?'

'Have you identified the thief?'

'Not yet, but—'

'Then I do not want to hear about it.'

Gussie gave a soft, sad sigh. 'How cruel you are. Utterly without heart, I am sure of it.'

'You look horrifying in this state, Miss Werth. I can hardly bear to look at you.'

She brightened at once. 'I do, don't I? How kind of you to say so!'

'You are most welcome. Now, why did you come to find *me*, and so soon? I imagine there is something I am to do for you.'

'I have news.'

He waited, but she was uncharacteristically shy about coming out with it. 'Well?'

'I have suffered a setback, on the topic of the thief. The thing is – well, I was robbed.'

'Of?'

'A set of pearls. I was wearing them around my neck, and then at some point I realised that I was not.'

'Yes, this thief is clever and light-fingered. When, and where, did you lose them?'

'In the card-room. I think? Last night. I had just been talking to one of the Mummers, a strange woman—'

'The Tudor Queen.'

'Yes! Oh, you have seen her as well. Did you find out who she is?'

'No. I was beginning to hope you were going to tell me.'

'I was interrupted before I could question her properly, and I never saw her again after.'

'A great pity. I imagine the delay in your bringing me these tidings can be accounted for by simple means: you were not planning to tell me at all, and then changed your mind.'

'How did you know?'

'I only need to imagine the most disgraceful, disreputable explanation possible, and I have it.'

Gussie smiled. 'I never knew you for such a flatterer, Mr. Ballantine.'

'Yes, I ought to have guessed you would see that as a compliment. Why, though, did you change your mind?'

'I came to my senses, and realised I had done wrong.'

Ballantine folded his arms. 'And the real reason?'

'I thought you might already know who that Tudor lady was, and thereby free me to work on a much more important problem.'

'That being?'

'Why, Frosty's death, of course.'

'Does Lord Maundevyle know how little you regret his passing?'

'Of course not, he is dead.'

'That poor man. I trust he will get over his tendre for you soon enough.'

'Yes, it is very odd of him, isn't it.' Gussie paused. 'Of course, when I speak of Frosty's death, I include Lord Maundevyle's, and all the rest of them—'

She stopped, because the door to the little dressing-room opened, and in came Theo. It cost Ballantine a moment's effort to recognise him, for he was much taller than usual, and all bulk. An ogre.

Gussie went off into a peal of mirth.

'Oh *no*,' Theo gasped. 'As if Great-Aunt Honoria were not bad enough!'

'Yes, I am resolved on being a complete terror. As, I see, are you.'

Theo fixed his unhappy gaze upon Ballantine. 'I don't suppose there is any way we can swap back, is there?'

'Believe me, I am enjoying this unaccustomed thirst as little as you are enjoying my brawn. If anybody can revert us, it would be Goodspeed, I suppose.'

'He will not, though,' Gussie put in. 'He is more like to send you off to do something shocking. I am told that is his purpose, as the Master of Misrule. He tells us to do things, and we must obey.'

'Insufferable,' muttered Theo, a sentiment with which Ballantine could not disagree.

'I am glad you are here, Theo,' continued Gussie, to that gentleman's palpable surprise.

'*Glad*? Me?'

'Yes, for I want your help with something. Yours, too, Mr. Ballantine.'

Ballantine eyed the lady with as much wariness as Lord Bedgberry. 'And what might that be?'

'We are to track down this mysterious Lord of the Palace – and the Lady, too, if indeed she exists – and beat him, or both of them, until they tell us what they have done to Frosty and how to reverse it.'

Ballantine thought back to the vision of dark Wyrde the Lord had presented, during the selection of Goodspeed as Master. 'Beat him,' he repeated.

'Beat him? Me?' said Theo.

'*You*, Theo, are the best placed of all of us to do so, having borrowed Mr. Ballantine's might.'

'And he is welcome to take it back,' growled Theo.

'So I would, if I could,' Ballantine answered. 'But not in order to perform violence upon the Lord of the Palace, Miss Werth. A more absurd notion I have never heard, and that is saying something, considering I have known *you* for some time now.'

'Then I will just have to do it myself,' sighed Gussie, and vanished.

'Oh, no,' said Theo.

Ballantine sighed. 'Do you suppose she will go after the man alone?'

'Of course she will. Gussie hasn't the sense of an infant.' Theo pulled at his hair. 'He will take her apart.'

'Bat her away like an irritating fly, more like.'

'Are you certain?'

Ballantine returned Theo's stare, conscience obliging him to say: 'No.'

Theo uttered a strangled howl of frustration. 'How like Gussie to take so freakish a notion into her head! As though we had not enough trouble on our hands already. We must find her.'

'In all likelihood she never left.' Ballantine felt it would be like Gussie, to vanish from view and loiter, secretly, listening to what they said about her after they thought she was gone.

But moments passed, as both gentlemen waited: silence.

'That was her moment to reveal herself, if ever there was one,' Theo said.

Ballantine sighed. 'Let us hope she has gone in search of other recruits, first. We may find her with her aunt, or perhaps with Miss Selwyn.'

'And where are they?'

'I have no idea.'

THE GENTLEMEN NEED NOT have worried, for Gussie's mad-cap venture proved as short-lived as it was ill-advised.

She wafted airily from Theo's chambers down to the lower floors, where she amused herself with visibility: how diverting were the shocked looks she received as she drifted daintily past, trailing rivulets of blood from her severed neck! Even in a house full of Wyrded wonders, no one quite expected to see a bodiless and bleeding head wander past. So diverting!

A great clamour came, still, from the vicinity of the feasting-room, and there Gussie turned her attention. Inside, she saw: a plethora of people seated at the tables, standing atop the tables, weaving among the tables in half-crazed dancing; none of whose antics interested her in the slightest, for she also saw, seated by herself in what passed for a quiet corner and engaged in consuming a cup of chocolate, Miss Frostell.

'Frosty?' she shouted, and swooped.

Her companion looked up as she approached, and smiled a little vaguely. 'Hello, my dear. How odd you look without the rest of your body, to be sure. I do hope you have left it somewhere you will remember to look, when you want to take it up again?'

'Frosty,' Gussie repeated, and attempted, without much success, to manifest her missing limbs. 'How came you to be here?'

'Oh! I must have overslept myself, for I woke so terribly hungry. I rang for a servant, but nobody came, so I thought it right to venture down. And there were such lovely things to be had! I am quite comfortable, now.'

Dinner had, indeed, been served while Gussie was gadding about the house. Could she eat as a revenant? Did she want to?

No matter. Frosty sat before her, her own, dear Frosty, and as long as she were *true* to herself, and fully restored, then all was right with the world. 'Do you feel... well, Frosty?'

'Now that I have had my dinner I feel very well. Though there is a trifle too much noise below stairs. I believe I will return to my own room, shortly.'

'You do not feel... oh, disordered? As though you might have been... ill.'

'Why, I have not been ill in years, my dear. Not properly, to speak of. Why do you ask? Do I look poorly?'

Gussie beamed upon her erstwhile governess, enchanted. 'No, *dear* Frosty. You look absolutely charmingly.' She did not look at all as though she had spent the greater part of a day dead: her appearance was as neat and ordered as ever, and a healthy enough colour put the roses into her cheeks.

'I am glad to hear you say so. It did strike me that you were a trifle worried, my dear, and that would be a pity at so grand a party.'

'Oh, I am very well *now*. You have relieved me of the solemn duty of committing murder, upon which I *had* fully resolved, until a moment ago. Now I may be easy, and enjoy myself.'

This announcement caught Miss Frostell's full attention, as it ought; one's charge does not often declare a practical interest in homicide, even if one's charge was Miss Augusta Werth. She looked up from her chocolate, and studied her protegee with closer attention. 'I hope it was not poor Lord Bedgberry you were planning to do away with? Though he can be a little thoughtless once in a great while, I am sure he does not deserve to die for it. And I cannot think it quite proper to be slaughtering one's own close relatives, my dear.'

'Slaughtering other people's, however, would be a different matter? I fully agree with you there.'

Poor Frosty turned the full weight of her gentle intellect onto Gussie's witticism, and considered it seriously. 'To be sure, there may be occasions where it is justified, but I cannot think what they might be.'

'I could, Frosty, and I did. But I shan't trouble you with the details. I will not be killing anybody tonight, it appears, and therefore I beg you not to worry yourself over it.'

'You relieve my mind greatly.'

Gussie felt an uncharacteristic stab of compunction. 'I believe I run you half ragged, do not I? I ought to take better care of you.' Her usual idea of good sense righted itself, after a moment's silent regret, and she added, 'And you ought not to concern yourself over me, for I always come right in the end.'

Miss Frostell took in the horrific sight of Gussie, freshly severed at the neck and bleeding, and said in her mild way: 'I daresay you do, my dear.'

CHAPTER FOURTEEN

APRIL 30TH

This book has been burning a hole in my pocket, I am sure of it. I felt a burning sensation, anyway, though when I took it out there was no damage to my clothes. It merely wanted to get my attention, I suppose, and so it has. It does that, if I do not write in it for too many hours together.

Not that I have had much leisure for writing, tonight. I have played the organ again, for a time – I do not even recall going into that room, must have walked there in a half-sleep, or some such thing – and then came the ridiculous Feast of Fools. I was stuffed into the costume of a cook, for a short period (the chef, even, I believe), and a more ridiculous notion I cannot imagine. Whoever heard of a chef that does not even eat? I would not have the first idea how to prepare so much as an omelette.

But that did not last long, for the Lord of we Fools appointed, in his wisdom, Goodspeed. And our dear Goodspeed soon betrayed every comfortable idea we had as to our safety in such hands, and began this "topsy-turvy" nonsense. I am become Ballantine, for tonight, or some semblance of him. My face, his Wyrde. He has my Wyrde, for a few hours, and I wish him joy of it.

Gussie has taken Great-Aunt Honoria's Wyrde, and is no doubt wreaking havoc all over the castle. At least Honoria cannot do much damage with Gussie's: everyone here is Wyrded already.

Something odd occurred not half an hour ago (something else, I should say, for everything being turnabout, there is no shortage of oddities). Ballantine and I were in search of Gussie's associates: my parents, perhaps, or Miss Selwyn, or even the Jendrings, with whom she seems to be thick as thieves at present. We found none of them, including (of course) Gussie: but I was almost sure, as we pushed our way down a corridor crowded with irritating merry-makers, that I saw Lord Maundevyle. I must have imagined it. He is, after all, dead, or something very like it.

It is possible Gussie is, too. She went off in search of the Lord of this wretched castle, he whose peculiar Wyrde grants him so much dangerous power over the inhabitants of this house. She had notions of threatening murder, as though that would do any good, and I rather think he will instead murder her.

Ballantine and I were obliged to give up the pursuit, finding no trace of her. If she is dead, then I suppose her remains will be delivered to us at some point, and my father will revive her. She did seem to be enjoying her sojourn as a revenant, so I do not suppose she will much mind the alteration.

I trust I have now penned sufficient reflections to satisfy my importunate book. Why, journal, do you harangue me so?

Asking questions of the book produced no response, of course, even though he penned his queries in ink on its own pages: no ghostly words shimmered into being in reply, nor did any answers materialise amidst his own thoughts, placed there by whatever mysterious Wyrde operated the journal.

He closed it up, and put it back into his pocket. He wore Ballantine's clothes at present, or some approximation of them: including capacious pockets, into which an Incident Book had many a time been tucked. His journal fitted nicely in there. How he had retained the book, when everything else about him had altered, he could not explain. He supposed the thing clung to him, and would not be parted by any effort or Wyrde.

His fingers were itching again, an odd sensation only appeased by returning to the distant chamber in which the organ reposed, and thundering away upon it until the strange urge quieted. Thither he turned his steps, upon leaving the study (a room arrayed for writing, with several tables equipped with pens and ink: he almost felt that the chamber had been put there on purpose, precisely for such journalling emergencies. But that was absurd. He was the only person in possession of such a book, was not he? And therefore the only person likely to employ the space).

His handwriting had emerged messily: gripping a pen in his thickened fingers proved challenging. He wondered how Ballantine managed to record anything in his Incident Book, when his ogre came upon him. Perhaps he didn't.

The passages slowly emptied as Theo paced along, growing, mercifully, quieter; most of the revellers were clustered around the feasting rooms, and the dancing, and few felt an interest in the more isolated parts of the house. He felt a degree of self-consciousness, travelling those long halls with such height and breadth to his frame, such pugnacious brawn about him. He attracted no such attention in his regular shape, not even when he had slipped at dinner, and got blood on his collar-points. Upon slipping into the chamber in which the organ slept, he found the space deserted, and sighed in relief.

Lamps flickered with bright flames along the walls, illuminating the vast and imposing bulk of the organ. It crouched there like some slumberous beast waiting to rouse, dark wood and glimmering silver, menace and majesty. Theo felt a kinship with it, a yearning to touch it, to run his thickened fingers over its smooth ivory keys and revel in its melodies.

So powerful an urge (and so uncharacteristic, he being, in a regular way, not at all musical) might have occasioned more remark, on any other day. But in this Wyrde and wondrous house, normal was a concept which held no meaning: Theo dismissed it.

He touched his clumsy fingers to the keys. The first few notes sounded, sending shivers through to his core; goosebumps rose on his skin. He smiled.

Tonight's melody proved different from his previous play-ings: softer, mournful, a touch of the lament about it. Perhaps it was because Miss Frostell was gone, and Lord Maundevyle, and all the others; perhaps a small, secret part of himself grieved.

Perhaps he simply mourned the loss of his Wyrde, temporary though it (hopefully) would prove. He had to concentrate in order to play properly – an ogre has no business with music, it is not his province. Every note crafted gently, with exquisite care, lest he make a mull of it—

—so intent was he on his music, and so powerful the mighty instrument's tones, he did not hear the door open, or the soft footsteps behind him, as somebody came in. Supposing there had even been such sounds to be heard; that the newcomer had not simply materialised at his elbow, for there, suddenly, she stood, a vision in velvet and ermine, and Theo started violently.

The music stopped.

'Madam,' he choked, swallowing. 'You startled me.'

He could not long keep from playing: already his fingers moved again, beginning a waltz, now, a lilting melody with a discordancy to it, something twisted in the tune. Perhaps it was the lady's smile that did it, for that, too, was twisted and sublime.

'I did,' she said, in a low voice of silk.

'I believe you enjoyed it,' replied Theo, in some disgust.

That smile widened; the glorious eyes, deep blue, twinkled with mirth and mystery. 'You play beautifully,' remarked the lady. 'Rarely has such music been heard in these halls.'

'I don't know how.' The melody veered deeper into discordancy, a dizzying descant added to the tune. 'I am not musical. I don't play the organ, my lady: it plays me.'

She studied him, intent. 'Then: the music reflects your moods. Something is amiss with you, tonight: you are half a cacophony.'

'I am wearing someone else's Wyrde, and it fits me ill.'

'But only slightly. Hearken: harmony prevails.'

She had reddish hair, this queen amongst women, arrayed like a lady at Elizabeth's Court. Her attire matched, a grand gown in layers of luxury, costly – and ancient. Theo's curiosity deepened.

'Who are you?' said he, bluntly. 'The Mummer's Dance ended some hours ago, ma'am.'

'Ah, but I am not a mummer.'

'So I perceive. What are you, then?'

'Something else.' Merriment brightened her glorious eyes, and mockery as well: Theo bristled.

'If you came here to torment me, I bid you go. I am occupied.' He turned his back to her, and devoted himself to the music.

'You seek a thief.'

These words reclaimed him, to his annoyance. He wrested his hands from the keys, and turned to her. '*I* do not, precisely, but I have been drawn into the business. Know you something of this thief?'

'I know everything of this thief. Would you have me enlighten you?'

'My cousin would, or Mr. Ballantine. I bid you seek *them* out, and leave me in peace.'

'But I would rather talk to you.'

'Why?'

An eyebrow rose; her eyes glittered. 'You interest me.'

'If it is the ogre in me that interests, then I bid you again seek Ballantine. The ogre, ma'am, belongs to him.'

'It is not the ogre.'

Theo began to feel impatient. 'What is it, then?'

'Yours is an unusual spirit.'

'I know that,' he muttered. 'I am not usually applauded for it.'

'Come with me.' The invitation tugged at his heart, spoken deep and low, laced with some strange, Wyrde power.

Theo took a step back. 'Oh, no. Not more of your mesmeric nonsense, if you please. I have had quite enough of *that*.'

The temptation faded: her majesty blinked. 'I do not compel you. You are free to decline.'

'Well, I am declining.'

He had irritated her at last: her eyes narrowed, her lips compressed to a thin line. 'You would find it more *entertaining* to come with me.'

'I am not very interested in those sorts of entertainments,' answered he, shortly.

She laughed, surprised. 'Are not you? That cannot be.'

Theo folded his arms, forming of them a physical barrier between him and the importunate lady. 'I will make you a counter offer, ma'am. Tell me honestly who you are, and I will consider your suggestion.'

'Declined.' Her smile was back, mocking once more.

'Then I direct you to my cousin, ma'am, as I said before, and bid you good evening.' Theo returned to his beloved organ, and began once more to play. The music emerged thunderously, laced with anger, spiky with irritation.

He did not see her leave, any more than he had seen her arrive. He only noted, with relief, that he was alone again, hopefully for good. No more gentle care with the keys for him: his thick fingers trampled the ivory, littering the melody with wrong, jagged notes. With his heart swelling with annoyance and his thoughts awhirl, Theo did not care.

SOMEONE ELSE HAD SPOTTED Lord Maundevyle, too. Gussie caught a glimpse of his brushed dark locks in the midst of the crowd in the ballroom; he was dancing, though she could not see with whom.

The demented organ-player was at it again, pounding away at some manner of waltz. The guests, delighted, had taken up the dance en masse. Gussie felt some surprise that Henry should prove so eager at it.

Ordinarily, pushing and shoving her way through the swarm to reach Henry's side would have posed considerable difficulty.

Now, she merely floated up and over the heads of the dancers, and swooped upon Henry from a great height.

He jumped, and stared, coming to a sudden halt in the midst of the dance. 'M-miss Werth!'

'I know! I have never looked so well in my life before, have I?' She beamed, wreathed in smiles just like Ivo. No wonder the man was so jolly! 'Haunting people is so satisfying. I believe I shall never know how to leave off doing it.'

Henry's partner glared daggers at Gussie. The girl was a little stout, and red in the face from exertion, though she had seemed capable enough as a dancer. 'My apologies,' Gussie told her, without much sincerity. 'Only, his lordship was dead and gone half an hour ago, so I found myself unusually desirous of his company now that he is not.'

'Unusually?' Henry appeared crushed.

'I would not normally be so rude about it,' Gussie hastened to add. 'What was it like, being dead?'

'I am sure I do not know. I feel as though I had only slept deeply, and could not have been more surprised when I woke. Everybody was staring at me as though they had seen a ghost.' He shuddered.

'Yes, well, do try not to die on us again for some time. Hm?'

'I was not given much choice in the matter the first time, but I can certainly attempt to carry out your command.' He bowed to Gussie, unconscious of his partner's aggravation; the girl threw up her hands, and stalked off.

'I would offer to partner you in place of the lady I have re-pelled, but as you can see I am short a few limbs tonight.'

Henry smiled. 'I thought Clarissa would kill me all over again, so great was her annoyance. She has not, I hope, taken out her murderous fury upon you?'

'Oh, no. This is simply Goodspeed's idea of a joke, and a fool's game it certainly is. Someone is wandering around with your Wyrde, I suppose, and I hope they will not do too much damage to the house while they are at it. Dragons are not made for enclosed spaces, as we have already learned.'

'I do not feel any different,' Henry answered.

'You have not manifested some Wyrde that is unusual for you?'

'Nothing.'

'Hm. Then Goodspeed's transformation, for you, was from death to life. I hope that does not imply that others have gone from living, to dead.'

'Or that I shall be deceased again once the Misrule is over.'

Gussie pursed her lips, arrested by that prospect. 'I had better talk to Goodspeed.'

'Pray do. I am attached to this life, and not yet ready to relinquish it.'

Gussie had other questions for the enigmatic Goodspeed, too. Fortunately, he did not prove difficult to discover. She simply withdrew to her chambers, and, once there, rang the bell.

Goodspeed's Wyrde was of a persuasive nature; when he suggested something to you, you saw his point immediately, and hastened to act upon it. This rendered him perfect for the role of butler. Whether he also possessed some preternatural sense that informed him when he was wanted, well, Gussie had her suspicions; ringing the bell seemed only a formality, for he appeared (as he so often did) very promptly indeed.

'Miss Werth?' said he, paused at the door to her chamber, and bowed.

'You ought not to bow today, I suppose,' she answered. 'Not in that outfit, anyway.'

Close up, he looked odd in the regalia of the Master of Misrule: so recognisable as her staid and sensible butler, yet thus arrayed. A strange incongruity. He knew it, too, for his smile was rueful.

'I remain your butler, Miss Werth, whatever my other duties may be tonight. Was there something with which I can assist you?'

'There are two things,' she said crisply. 'Firstly: I thank you for waving your sceptre there and restoring Frosty and Lord Maundevyle, and you are not to reverse the procedure, if you please. I want them where they are supposed be: breathing.'

'I will do my best, but these are borrowed powers. I shall not hold them for much longer.' He paused, some uncertainty crossing his normally imperturbable features. 'In truth, I am not at all certain that their restoration owes anything to my intervention at all.'

'Then have a word with his peculiar lordship, on my behalf. Tell him if he does not restore everyone to their proper place by the end of the masque – including the deceased persons – then I shall be removing his head.'

'Very good, Miss.'

'As for the other thing.' Gussie gestured the butler inside, and closed the door after him. 'You are aware, I imagine, that we have been some little time in pursuit of a thief?'

'I have heard a word or two on the subject, yes.'

'Trying to intercept such a person in this much chaos is a hopeless business. I have made no progress at all, save to lose my own pearls. And *then* I was distracted by Frosty's demise, and now I find myself falling behind. Which will never do, for I was so foolish as to inform Mr. Ballantine of the fact, and I shall lose his respect altogether if I do not come about.'

'How would you like me to assist you, Miss?' said the faithful Goodspeed.

'For one thing, all the bedchambers in this house must be searched. If the thief is here, and I believe he or she *is*, then they have been having a field day in all this mess. Their rooms must be overflowing with jewels. You have a way with the servants: will you arrange it? I could not hope to get through so many chambers by myself, nor even with Clarissa's help.'

'I believe I can manage that, Miss, yes.'

'Excellent. And one other thing. I believe the thief to have been hiding behind the façade of a Tudor Queen, as Mr. Ballantine puts it, but I cannot find out who she is underneath the mask. I encountered her during the Mummer's Dance.'

'I will make enquiries,' Goodspeed promised.

'Thank you, Goodspeed.' Gussie beamed. 'You may go.'

'There is one more thing, Miss Werth.'

Gussie looked an enquiry.

The butler raised his silver sceptre: it glittered oddly in the light. 'I am the Master of Misrule, and I will not leave you without requiring something of you.'

'Why must I perform some forfeit? I have been everything that is charming.'

'You have asked something of me. Now I shall ask something of you.'

Gussie felt a deepening sense of foreboding. 'And I must obey. Is that not how this works?' Though Goodspeed hardly required the powers of Misrule to oblige her to comply; he was persuasive enough without them.

'I believe so, Miss. Are you ready?'

'No!'

His smile was faint. 'My command to you is this: show your journal to your cousin.'

Gussie blinked. 'My journal? To Theo? Whatever for?'

'Mine is not to explain, mine is only to command.' With which maddening statement, and accompanying twinkle of his eyes, Goodspeed bowed and took himself off.

Gussie mulled over his peculiar directive. She had expected something more – shocking, perhaps, or scandalous; something befitting the merriment and the madness of the party. As far as that went, Goodspeed's choice of task relieved her mind.

But befuddlement remained. What possible interest could Theo take in her journal? Was it the contents she was supposed to show him? Why? She could imagine his disgust: a world full of books of scholarly interest at his disposal, and she desired him to read her own, pointless scrawl!

Still, she would obey Goodspeed in this, because she must. Anyway, the worst Theo could do was laugh at her, and scorn her efforts at prose: she was equal to such treatment as that, having endured it for much of her life.

'Odd,' she said aloud, and wafted off.

CHAPTER FIFTEEN

MR. BALLANTINE'S CONCERN FOR Gussie did not fade either so quickly or so completely as her cousin's had. He maintained the search for her for over an hour, without effect, and ended his efforts at last at the side of Lord and Lady Werth.

The two were enjoying a comfortable coze in a majestic conservatory, a long walk and many winding passages from the ballroom and the dining chamber. Lady Werth sat at her elegant ease upon a low bench, surrounded by fragrant greenery; opposite to her sat Lord Werth. The latter did not turn as Ballantine approached, but his lady wife smiled a welcome upon the Runner.

'Ah, Mr. Ballantine. We have not seen a great deal of each other, have we? I trust you have been enjoying the festivities.'

'Something like that, my lady,' said Ballantine, vaguely. He added nothing more, for upon approaching their lord and ladyship's little arbour he all but tripped over the third member of their company: Victor Daundelyon, laid out on the floor at Lady Werth's feet. The man lay with his white face turned up to the ceiling, eyes staring, his body rigid as a board: stone dead.

'Oh,' said Ballantine, and stopped.

'I see you are enjoying a taste of my son's Wyrde,' said Lady Werth, smiling upon his changed appearance. 'So odd a notion of our dear Goodspeed's, though I confess, the experience is not without its points of interest.'

'And Daundelyon?' Ballantine gestured.

'I have been testing my husband's Wyrde on the poor man. I had hoped that, with an exchange of wielder, perhaps the arts might prove more effective. But of course, they have not.'

Ballantine sank down upon the bench beside her ladyship. From this vantage point, he enjoyed a clearer view of Lord Werth: the older gentleman sat still as a statue, his skin coated in a fine layer of ice.

'My poor husband has enjoyed no greater success with my Wyrde, than I with his,' confided Lady Werth, with a little laugh. 'He will thaw out in an hour or two, I daresay.'

'Aye, well. You have had a lifetime to accustom yourself to it. He, but an hour. What happened to Victor, ma'am? Did he meet with some manner of accident?'

'Oh, the same as all the others, I believe. Though of more recent date. I saw him alive and well only a few hours ago.'

'Before the Feast of Fools began?'

'Yes. Another strange notion of Goodspeed's, I imagine.'

Ballantine thought rapidly. Goodspeed had declared a night of "topsy-turvy", deeming the change-about between master and servant insufficient revelry. He had caused most people's Wyrde to change about with that of another; had he also caused those who were dead to rise, and others who lived to change places with *them*?

If so, that explained Daundelyon's present state, and offered the appealing possibility of a reversal of it, later.

It also suggested that, somewhere about the castle, the befuddling Miss Jendring might be presently stirring once again.

'You have not seen Gussie, I suppose?' he asked, remembering the nature of the errand that had brought him into the conservatory.

'Not this evening.'

'She has got Lady Honoria's Wyrde, and is enjoying herself altogether too much with it.'

'Then she is well entertained.'

Ballantine coughed. 'Erm. I hardly know how to tell your ladyship, but she spoke of plans to—murder someone. The Lord of this house, specifically.'

'Well, if she is tired afterwards I hope she will have the sense to go to bed early. But the young have so little idea of their own good, and Gussie less than most; I hardly dare to hope she will take so sensible a step.'

Ballantine, silenced, could only stare. 'Ah,' he said at length, recovering himself. 'If you are not concerned, Lady Werth, then I will endeavour to follow your example.'

'It is of no use to be concerned about Gussie,' she said, crisply. 'One will only wear oneself into an early grave, and my dear husband would be so very cross with me, if I did that.'

She was in the right of it, reflected Ballantine. Gussie was enough to drive anybody to an early death.

Ballantine, on the point of excusing himself, began to rise; Lady Werth prevented him with a few words. 'Oh, Mr. Ballantine, while you are here: about your thief.'

He sat again at once. 'Oh? You have discovered something.'

'Earlier this evening I was sitting with Lady Alicia. She has lost her diamonds, you know. I believe the loss occurred yesterday, during the Mummering.'

'Lady Alicia Greaves. Yes, I came upon her myself not long after they were stolen.'

'Ah, then you know all about it already.' Lady Werth, abandoning the subject, took up the cup of tea that waited at her elbow, and sipped.

'I should like to hear whatever it was your ladyship thought to tell me, nonetheless. Lady Alicia spoke, perhaps, of the mummer I saw leaving the room, shortly afterwards? The lady dressed like Queen Elizabeth.'

'I know little of that; she hardly mentioned the matter to me. But she had not been enjoying a solitary half-hour, Mr. Ballantine, as I do; a less solitary creature than Alicia I can scarcely imagine. No, she had been in conversation with several other ladies, and it was only after they had gone away again that she noticed the absence of her jewels.'

'Several other ladies,' echoed Ballantine. 'But not including the queen?'

'I believe not. Whoever she was – perhaps she was only passing through.'

The loss of what had seemed a sound theory was not unlike feeling solid ground turn to quicksand under your feet; the world shifted around you, leaving you floundering. Ballantine heartily disliked the sensation. 'And who were these other ladies, ma'am?'

'Let me see.' Lady Werth took a slow sip of tea. 'Mary Fortescue, I believe, poor old soul. Ought to have been dead and gone this past century at least, but no amount of effort can render her otherwise than alive – in a manner of speaking, that is. A trying Wyrde.' Sip. 'Mrs. Maybury. I should think her far too rich to be a jewel thief, however. She could buy Werth Towers six times over, and barely notice.' A longer sip of tea, then; a moment's thought. 'Lady Tantony, about whom I know nothing whatsoever. But to look at her, one could easily imagine her engaged in something so roguish as robbery. Quite the engaging bandit.'

Lady Werth fell silent long enough that Ballantine ventured to ask: 'Was that all?'

'There was one more, but the details elude me. One of the Jendring girls, at any rate; I forget which.'

Jendring. That name arrested Ballantine's attention, and not merely because he recognised it: he sat up.

'I saw a Miss Jendring, myself,' he remembered. 'Not long after Lady Alicia's diamonds were taken. I bumped into her, below-stairs.' And something about that meeting had bothered him ever since; something the lady had said, perhaps? But he could not pin down the thought.

'They are not a poor family, the Jendrings, but they are far from rich.' Lady Werth finished her tea, and set down her cup. 'I know no actual harm of them.'

'Thank you, ma'am,' said Ballantine sincerely. The information may prove to be nothing at all, but then again, it might not. At least he had a direction for his enquiries.

She looked at him rather penetratingly. 'How are you getting on with Theo's Wyrde?'

'I am – hungry, ma'am.' The thirst was like a claw clutching at his throat, and slowly tightening. It cost him a constant effort to ignore it.

Lady Werth patted his hand. 'I should go down to the kitchens, if I were you, and enquire if they have got anything suitable. It is the elegant solution.'

Ballantine recoiled from the notion of quaffing blood from a cup, but as a solution, it was indeed far more elegant than his falling upon some hapless person's neck, as Miss Jendring had done with him. 'I'll try that,' he agreed, and rose.

TRACKING DOWN THE ELUSIVE and irascible Lord Bedgberry proved no easy task. Gussie reflected, with some disgust, that she had spent half the festivities trying to find someone or other in the chaos, usually without success. She searched the dancers and the diners, without any luck; swooped through Theo's rooms, and every library or book-room she could find; wandered the passages like a forlorn ghost, popping through the walls into every chamber she passed, and still failed to discover him. And throughout, that demented organ music! Would it never *stop*?

Worse, her search was drawing her, inexorably, nearer and nearer the source of that music, for as she drifted on and on, the music grew louder and louder.

At last she entered the vaulted, shadowy chamber in which the detested instrument resided, and saw: a hulking figure, impossibly tall, hunched over the keys, transported by the violently cacophonous music pouring from his fingers.

'Mr. Ballantine!' cried Gussie. 'I had not known you to be musical! And I must own, I wish rather that you were not.'

She had to shout to be heard over the tumult, and thought for a moment that she had not been. But the sounds of her voice penetrated the fog of composition eventually: Ballantine's head jerked up, and he stopped playing. He turned, and the expression of rage on his contorted features might have appalled her, were it not for a much more disturbing realisation.

'Theo!'

'Can a man not be left to play in *peace*?' snarled Lord Bedgberry.

Gussie, torn between anger and mirth, had nothing to say. That the detestable and detested organ-player should turn out to be Theo! Of all people! She could wring his infernal *neck* for taking up so abominable a pastime.

But the sight of his features — stretched uncomfortably over the broad face of an ogre! And him standing so awkwardly, like a schoolboy in short trousers – too, *too* diverting.

'Oh dear, Theo,' she said, giving way to laughter. 'How uncomfortable you must be.'

Theo tugged at the cuffs of his shirt, as though pulling them down might better conceal the length and bulk of his arms. 'I do not know how Ballantine can stand it.'

'I suppose he stands it because he must. I do not suppose he is enjoying *your* Wyrde any better.'

'No doubt. When we get our hands on Goodspeed, he is like to come off rather badly.'

'But he is so useful, Theo. Do not damage him too badly, I beg you.'

'If I am permitted to play uninterrupted,' said Theo coolly, 'I tend to be in a better humour.'

'But what on earth are you doing playing an organ? You never touched a piano a day in your life.'

Theo shrugged, and turned back to the keys. He touched his thick fingers to a few of them, playing a softer, lilting melody. 'I cannot explain it any better than you can, cousin.'

'Well, I will leave you to play in peace in a moment, and you may take that as a high compliment, for I utterly detest the music.'

'Thank you.'

'But I am sent on an errand from Goodspeed, and, you know, he cannot be refused.'

She saw, rather than heard, Theo sigh; his big shoulders dropped. 'All right, what is it?'

'I am instructed to show you something.' Gussie fished up the journal, from wherever her pocket ought to be: she had lastingly mislaid her legs, but the book would not permit itself to remain long out of reach. 'Here,' she said.

Theo took the book, frowning. He turned it over, opened it, read a few lines, and looked up at her. 'I don't understand. What is this?'

'I had hoped you might know. Goodspeed seemed certain that you would.'

He delved into a pocket of his own, and retrieved a book of similar size, with a red cover. 'I had not thought to take up journalling, either, but I admit I find it rewarding. Clears the thoughts. Perhaps Goodspeed meant for you to recommend the pursuit to me, but if so, he is behindhand.'

Gussie stared at the books, matching in size and proportion, if not in hue. 'I saw you with that once before,' she said. 'At dinner. Theo. Had it only just then come into your possession?'

'I believe so. I have not had it long.'

'Why, I have not had mine long. It was sent to me, by some anonymous donor, in a parcel.'

Theo frowned at her. 'I found mine outside my door, wrapped in paper, with no notion as to the sender.'

'Then we are both in possession of journals sent by unknown persons. Does yours do anything... odd?'

'Oh, it wandered about a bit at first, but I have not known it to do so lately.'

Gussie raised her eyes heavenwards. 'Theo. For several days you have had a book in your grasp that *wanders about under its own power*, and you never thought to mention it to any of us?'

'Why, does not yours do the same?'

Gussie thought, a little guiltily, of one occasion some few days past. She had gone into her room and found the book lying on her dressing-table, when she remembered leaving it on her nightstand. She had concluded that she'd simply forgotten, and thought nothing of it. 'It may. I haven't confirmed it. But oh, Theo, it calls to me in some odd fashion. If I do not write in it for a day, or even for half a day, it—'

'Itches,' said Theo. 'Yes.'

'So. Whatever they are, they are the same, and must come from the same place.'

Theo's fingers tightened around his book, as though Gussie might be planning to take it from him. 'Mine has never harmed me. It isn't like the – other Books.'

'I very much hope it is not, indeed. But just because it has not harmed you yet – or mine, me – does not mean that it will not. Remember Mrs. Daventry's Book? It was as good as gold for years, until it wasn't.'

'Yet, you have kept yours.'

'I am grown rather fond of it, though I know I should not be.'

'Yes.' Theo slipped his journal back into his pocket, and returned Gussie's to her. 'Are there any other such books among the family?'

'Not to my knowledge. Or Goodspeed's, either, or I feel sure he would have sent me off after those as well.'

'If my book does anything else untoward, I shall be sure to mention it.'

'As shall I.' Gussie contented herself with that, feeling that she had discharged her errand from Goodspeed with honour. 'I suppose you will go on playing now, will you?'

'If I am not interrupted yet *again*.' He glowered.

'Come, Theo, one interruption even you could bear, if you tried.'

'But it has not been just one.' Theo turned back to his beloved organ, and began playing a gentle waltz.

'A good choice. The dancers will be delighted with you: they liked the waltz above anything.'

Theo did not answer, and Gussie withdrew. She had spent quite enough of her evening dashing thither and yon, and had thoughts of settling down by Frosty, perhaps with a cup of chocolate.

WHEN GUSSIE RETURNED TO the ballroom, however, she found the dancing over, for Goodspeed was holding court. A high dais at one end of the cavernous chamber held The Master of Misrule's throne, in which sat the Master himself, surrounded by attendants. The Wyrde and Wondrous formed a swarm packed closely together in a ring around the room; though very large, the ballroom still struggled to contain so many hundreds of guests all together. A space in the heart of the chamber was yet left clear: some kind of pageant was in progress, the players for which included Mr. Portman and, rather to Gussie's surprise, Hayton.

She had missed too much of the story to pick up the thread of it now. Hayton wore a crown of silver tinsel, and a purple gown. The pageant was mimed rather than spoken; Gussie arrived in time to see Hayton crossing the makeshift stage with queenly step, chin held very high, while Mr. Portman and others grovelled at her feet.

Gussie bypassed the spectacle, and swooped down upon the butler.

'Goodspeed!' she whispered.

He did not turn his head. 'My dear Miss Werth, you address the Master of Misrule at this moment.'

'True, and proper etiquette is everything. Very well: my Lord Misrule, may I have your attention?'

He smiled, then, and ignored the pageant in her favour. 'You return, flushed with success, I perceive.'

'Well, I showed my journal to Theo, at any rate, and saw his in return. What I want to ask *you*, is: how did you know the two books were the same? And what else do you know about them?'

'If you ask something of me I must ask something of you.'

'You may do so by all means, only pray make it an enjoyable mission this time. Theo snarled at me with unwonted viciousness.'

'Very well, I shall find you a more congenial target for your next predations. Your questions first: I knew about your book because it was brought, first, to me, and you opened it in my presence.'

'That much I recall.'

'I knew about Lord Bedgberry's because Lord Silvester told me of it.'

Gussie's brain reeled. 'Silvester? *He* knew of it? And how did he contrive to tell you anything at all, at least with any clarity?'

'Silvester can be perfectly conversable, if one understands how to comprehend him.'

'A trick I wish you would share with the rest of us, but very well. And my other question?'

'I *know* little else about them. I *suspect* one or two things more, but I have, as yet, no proof.'

'Therefore, you are not going to tell me.'

'Not at this time, Miss Werth. I should hate to prejudice your thinking in an incorrect direction.'

Gussie eyed him sourly. 'I do not feel I have gained much real information, and yet I have promised you another forfeit.'

'A lesson has been learned today, then: be careful when making deals.'

'Be careful when making deals with *you*, certainly, though whether it is Goodspeed who proves so slippery, or the Master of Misrule, I have not yet determined.'

He smiled at that. The pageant drew to a close, and the guests whistled and applauded; Hayton, smiling, took several bows.

'It grows late,' observed Gussie. 'Misrule must soon be over, I think.'

'So it must, but we shall have some revelry yet.' The Master of Misrule rose from his throne, and lifted his sceptre. A pale ghost-light shone forth, and amplified his voice when he spoke. 'Ladies and Gentlemen of the Wyrde, I thank you for your entertainments! I have been most merrily diverted.'

A chorus of cheers and whistles: Gussie rolled her eyes.

'Our night of revelry draws soon to a close, but there is yet time for one final amusement. What will you have? A dance?'

Some cheering and clapping: moderate interest.

'Another pageant?'

Less enthusiasm: the applause waned.

'A game! A charade, perhaps – no! I have it. The hour of forfeits is upon us!'

A roar of approval, somewhat to Gussie's astonishment. A great golden vase erupted from the floor, and turned slowly there in the centre, filled to the brim with scraps of silver paper. One wafted up from the mass of written forfeits, and descended into Goodspeed's hands.

'I have a forfeit to be performed!' cried he. 'Mary Fortescue.'

Someone gave a whoop of a laugh: the ancient lady with whom Gussie had earlier conversed. 'Come, then, Master, I am ready!' she cackled.

'We seek Counsel from one so aged,' boomed Goodspeed. 'Come, advise your fellows. Choose one upon whom to bestow the wisdom of your vast experience.'

Mary Fortescue narrowed her eyes, her mirth vanishing in an instant. 'All that glitters is not gold, they say. She who risks all for finery will rue and rue again.'

The guests quieted: all sensed the current of menace beneath her words. No piece of merriment, this.

Gussie scanned the faces of all those she saw – the ladies, in particular. Mary spoke of gold, of finery, of risk: could she be speaking of the jewel thief?

Nobody obliged her by betraying a flash of guilt or compunction, but the chamber, so over-filled with guests, could hide a thief anywhere in its midst.

A second silverish scrap of paper floated into Goodspeed's grasp. 'A forfeit for Jack Madding!' he called, and a very tall young man with a red, laughing face stepped forward. 'Bow to the prettiest, kneel to the wittiest, and kiss the one you love best,' directed Goodspeed.

Jack Madding experienced no difficulty in identifying the right lady for such attentions. He promptly took the hand of the girl standing next to him – a short, plump, pretty creature with dark hair and a ravishing smile – and bowed over it. He knelt to her, then kissed her soundly; both came away laughing and rosy-cheeked.

'Ah,' sighed Gussie. 'How sweet.'

Goodspeed eyed her sideways. 'I suspect you of satire, Miss Werth,' he murmured, *sotto voce.*

'Oh, dear. And I perceive I am to be punished for it.'

The Master's smile was more of a smirk: Gussie judged herself correct. When the third forfeit drifted into his hands, she was in no way surprised to hear him announce: 'A forfeit for Gussie Werth!'

'Oh, very well,' she sighed.

'A kiss!' he proclaimed.

'What?' Gussie gasped.

'For a gentleman brave and loyal, whose heart (were the truth known) may already be lost to our fair lady's charms!'

'Goodspeed,' Gussie hissed. 'You had better not be speaking of Henry. You could not be so cruel.'

Goodspeed ignored her. 'I speak, of course, of the thief-taker, bane of criminals of all stamps: Hugh Ballantine.'

Gussie, too thunderstruck to think, let alone speak, maintained an appalled silence.

As did Ballantine, at least for several long moments. Then, over the flutter of laughter and cheers from the crowd, Gussie distinctly heard him say: 'I *beg* your pardon?'

'You have entirely lost your wits,' Gussie said, attempting to collect herself. '*Ballantine*? You must be mad.'

Goodspeed merely watched her, calm and unmoved, a glimmer of amusement lurking in his wise old eyes.

'I cannot be expected to kiss *anybody* in this state,' she protested, a touch hysterically.

'A fair argument,' Goodspeed conceded. 'But Misrule draws to a close: let your time of topsy-turvy be ended.' He shook his silver sceptre, and for a horrible instant Gussie felt *very* strange indeed.

When the twisting, squeezing, shuddersome sensations were over, she stood on her own two feet again, firm of figure and hale.

From somewhere in the crowd came Great-Aunt Honoria's voice: 'At last! I have not spent so interminably *dull* an evening this age at least!' And there she was, a disembodied head once more, weaving unsteadily up to the ceiling in demented celebration.

Gussie watched her progress a little sadly. 'Well, and what if I were to refuse this forfeit?' she said to Goodspeed. 'You cannot make me perform it.'

'I cannot,' Goodspeed agreed. 'And there will be no penalty should you refuse, Miss Werth. Misrule is not about torment. However.'

'However?'

'I wish you would believe me when I tell you: I do have your best interests at heart.'

'And Ballantine's?' riposted Gussie tartly.

'His, also.'

'You cannot be serious. This is some manner of prank.'

Goodspeed made no answer. He only said: 'Shall you take the forfeit, or shall I assign you another?'

Another. If she were to refuse this one, what horrors might Goodspeed come up with next?

Gussie sighed, and stepped down from the dais. The crowd parted before her, clearing a channel straight to Ballantine's side.

And there he was, restored to his own, familiar self. The reassuring solidity of him, strength and calmness combined. Eyes blue, piercing, and cold. Though – had she long known it? – they tended to warm when they rested on Gussie, even if it was with exasperation as much as any other feeling. His dark hair uncommonly disordered, tonight, and shadows under his eyes: he had been under some strain. He stared at her as she approached, more in horror than in tenderness; something deep inside Gussie flinched.

'Come,' said she. 'In the spirit of revelry, shall we get it over with?'

Heckling from the crowd: the spectacle was proving a disappointment.

Struck by a surge of mischief, Gussie grinned. She stepped up to the Runner; whispered, 'After all, I *have* made it my business to torment you, have not I?' and kissed him soundly.

The scent of him briefly overwhelmed her senses, familiar, masculine, solid. He did not move, and in a moment Gussie was dancing away again, laughing through the odd flutter of her heart.

The crowd, gratified, cheered, and Goodspeed went on to the next forfeit. Gussie did not look back at Mr. Ballantine; she did not want to see how he truly felt about what she had done. She feared that it might, in some unaccountable way, crush her.

DAY 3: MASQUERADE

CHAPTER SIXTEEN

MAY 1ST

Beltane, and the final day of the Masquerade is upon us. Or, rather, night, for what do any of us do in the lighted hours, but sleep? Such a schedule suits me admirably: I shall be sorry, in a sense, to return to London.

I played upon the organ deep into the night – would have played until dawn, by preference, though there came at last the striking of that infernal gong, several times, hard enough to shake the walls. When the disturbance stopped, my beloved organ shut itself up, like a door. Not a single note more could I draw from its burnished pipes.

Away went I to bed, and what tales of nonsense and absurdity have I had to hear this morning! Pranks and forfeits and pageants and I know not what. I say again: whatever can Goodspeed be thinking of?

CHARLOTTE E. ENGLISH

Still, his reign as Master of Misrule must now be over, and the chief of the foolishness with it, I trust. According to Great-Aunt Honoria, it is the Masquerade Ball that always falls on the last night of the event. Dancing and dominos, masks and music: civilised enough. Gussie says I shall not be excused from the dancing. We will see about that.

Following my odd conversation with Gussie about the journals (Goodspeed's fault, again), I have subjected my book to greater scrutiny, in hope of discovering some hitherto overlooked clue. No luck. I have even asked it a few questions, and what a fool I feel for interrogating a set of bound pages and expecting a response. I did not receive one, of course. The cursed thing remains enigmatic. I hope it is not preparing to turn savage, and maul me to death in my sleep. I would have to destroy it, then, and what a waste of effort that would be. I believe I have filled at least twenty pages already. (Do you hear this, Journal? I pray you, take note).

I reposed myself in my own rooms for slumber, and here I remain. I slept through the whole of the day, for night shrouds this castle once more. I sit at my window, still in my dressing-gown; it seems too great an effort to dress. I did not know that enjoying oneself could be so tiring.

Hunger drove Theo at last from his rooms, and down to the kitchens in search of relief. He had presented himself there before, and been promptly served: indeed, he had been invited to ring for another meal, when he chose to take it. But last night's debauchery had been so general, and so exhausting, as to overwhelm the servants as well, for nobody answered when he rang.

The kitchens, in contrast to the silent halls he passed through, were a riot of activity. Little was yet cooking, but heaped piles of prepared and chopped vegetables stood ready upon the enormous central table, and several cooks busied themselves with mounds of pastry and fruit.

'I take it there's to be another grand feast, is there?' said Theo, to the nearest of them.

She looked up, startled. 'Oh, Lord Bedgberry,' she said, and added, 'Bother.'

He saw that she was the same maid he had encountered before. She'd served him blood from a neat little cup, that time; today, she set down her knife, impatiently unbuttoned her cuff, and shoved her sleeve up to her elbow. 'Here,' she said, and handed him her wrist. 'I'm that sorry, but I've not time to serve it proper-like.'

Theo gingerly took the proffered hand, swallowing. How uncouth, to sup straight from the wrist, and she a servant, too! But he was ravenously hungry...

Mercifully, someone intercepted him before he could succumb. 'Here,' said another maid, and thrust a covered bowl into his hands. 'Already had to send up a supply for the Jendrings, but madam didn't want it.'

'Miss Fanny sent it back down, did she?' said the maid who had offered him her wrist.

'Aye, as usual, but look at that. Still full, almost to the brim. Her idea of a joke, belike.'

Theo relinquished the maid's delicate wrist with relief, and retired into a corner with his bowl. The contents proved fresh and fragrant: he did not wish to think too hard about who might have provided the refreshment, and devoted himself to imbibing it. Once done, he felt much revived, and set down the bowl in much better spirits.

'Jendrings,' he mused, at leisure now to think. Yes, the eldest Miss had a Wyrde like his own. Had not she been among the deceased, however? If she had been revived, temporarily, for Misrule, ought not she to be expired again? Theo shook his head. Too much topsy-turvy; he grew hopelessly muddled with it.

A thought filtered through, or rather, a question. Something he had heard failed to make sense, but he experienced a nagging sensation that it ought to.

He returned to the obliging maid, who greeted him with an exasperated sigh. 'Forgive me, my lord, but we are very busy.'

'I understand. Just a moment. What did you mean when you said "Miss Fanny sent it back down"?'

'Why, the bowl, sir. The one you was just drinking out of.'

'Yes, but why was it Miss Fanny who sent it back down, and not Miss Jendring, the eldest?'

'Oh! Well sir, it's the eldest as has got the more interesting Wyrde. The younger ones don't have much to speak of, though Miss Fanny makes herself useful on occasion, at least. She causes things to move about, sir, if I understand it rightly. She don't even need to touch them, I suppose.' She laughed, and added, 'Mind you, I wouldn't mind a Wyrde like that in my job. Would make clearing the pots ever so easy.'

'You do not call that interesting? I would.'

'She can't move things very far, sir, and if you've seen it done once, you've seen it a thousand times.'

'I daresay.' Theo left the girl to her work, musing. He saw the maid's point, to a degree: while Miss Fanny Jendring's Wyrde would make an amusing parlour trick when pouring the tea, there seemed little else she could do with it. Mind you, at least it was of some use, unlike his; why people persisted in seeing a Wyrde of his sort, or Miss Jendring's, as in some way glamorous he would never understand.

He stopped on his way back upstairs, wondering.

"She don't even need to touch them, I suppose."

Just how far could Miss Fanny Jendring move an object, and how close did she need to be to it herself in order to accomplish it?

Did she need to be able to see it – or only to know where it was?

Pertinent questions, all. Theo continued his journey upstairs, but this time, his steps were turned towards the comfortable parlour, where he hoped to find (in addition to Daundelyon, Hayton and Goodspeed), one Hugh Ballantine.

BALLANTINE AWOKE WITH A fresh resolution clear in his aching and befuddled head: he would never, ever drink again.

He had made such a resolution before, of course, and been (on occasion) tempted nonetheless to break it. He had done so last night, though in his own defence he had not been short of reasons.

Gussie Werth. The minx had avoided him since the forfeit, which was fortunate; it saved him the trouble of having to avoid her. They were bound to encounter each other soon, however. He resolved on behaving with scrupulous correctness, and making no reference at all to the kiss she had bestowed upon him.

He shook his head, halfway through slathering butter on a fresh roll. Of all the mad things he might have expected Gussie to do, kissing him – kissing *him!* – would never have entered his head. And all because the Master of Misrule had put her up to it. If it had not been for that, then she would never have done so, of course: he would do well not to read anything into it. What Goodspeed could have imagined himself about in putting the idea into her head – well. Ballantine had not yet had the courage to enquire.

He had the parlour all to himself, the hour being, relatively, early – dark outside, but with glimmers of the sunset still lingering on the horizon. His fellow guests were waking, one by one, and finding their way to breakfast, or having trays brought up: he heard footsteps passing his door several times, though mercifully no one had yet come in. He needed an hour at least, and a great deal more food and water, before he would be fit for company again.

He was not to remain long undisturbed, alas, for a mere half-hour's peaceful reverie proved to be his lot: he was interrupted, then, by a neat-figured, dark-haired hurricane, who swept in already in full flow.

'Mr. Ballantine! I do apologise for disturbing you so early, but you see, I have news.'

Gussie. Of all people, did his first social encounter of the morning have to be Gussie? He groaned inwardly, and put his face into his hands. 'No. Miss Werth, I beg of you, go away. At least until my head has left off aching so.'

'I would,' she said, more gently, and (unusually) with no trace of mockery. 'Only it is important.'

He sighed, and sat up, composing his face into a stern and quelling frown before he turned to face her. 'Very well. What is it?'

She smiled at him, looking annoyingly young and fresh for a woman who had, like himself, been carousing all night. 'I hope you slept well?'

'Perhaps we could get straight to the news, Miss Werth.'

'I do feel you ought to call me Gussie. After all—'

'*Miss* Werth. If you please.'

'Well then, it is this: I asked Goodspeed to arrange a search of everybody's rooms, and—'

'You did what?'

'I asked him to search the bedchambers,' Gussie repeated. 'For signs of my pearls, you know, or any of the other missing jewellery.'

'And in the process, alerting the thief to our pursuit.'

'Not at all. Goodspeed asked the maids, and they were very well able to do it while they were making up the rooms. Nobody has had cause to suspect a thing, I assure you.'

Ballantine only grunted, by no means pacified. 'Well, go on. What did this ill-advised search turn up?'

Gussie smiled again, like a child at Christmas, and produced from behind her back: a necklace of fine, pinkish pearls. 'This. Also a set of diamonds, *very* grand. Most likely they are Lady Alicia's: I am sure I have seen them before. And there is a brooch with rubies in it, and a pair of emerald earrings.'

Ballantine, wide awake now, stared at the pearls in her slim-fingered hands. 'So you have found the thief,' he said slowly. 'And who, pray, was it?'

'Well, we do not quite know that, *yet*. They were discovered in an airing cupboard in between several of the bedchambers: Mary Fortescue's is one, and Mrs. Wallis, and the Jendrings are all housed nearby.'

Mary Fortescue, and the Jendrings: Lady Werth had mentioned both names, when she had spoken of Lady Alicia's associates. 'Mrs. Fortescue,' he said slowly. 'She spoke of gold, at the forfeits, and issued a warning about it.'

'I think perhaps she knows, or guesses, who the thief is. She may have seen one of the Jendrings concealing the jewels, though if she did I cannot think why she did not come to you about it.'

'Not everybody knows who I am,' he pointed out. 'Or has such faith in me as you appear to.'

'If they do not, they ought to.' She was smiling upon him again: his gaze met hers, and held, until he flushed and looked away.

'You flatter me, Miss Werth.'

'Gussie.'

'That cannot be proper, and no, I will not be argued into it.'

Gussie took this with unwonted serenity, and he eyed her suspiciously. So kittenish a temper in so wild a woman could only bode ill. 'You are planning something. I can feel it.'

'I had some thoughts of speaking to the Jendrings,' she admitted.

The Jendrings. The thought he had been seeking – the elusive thought he could not pin down, since his unlucky and bloody encounter with the eldest Miss Jendring two nights past – struck him all at once. 'That's it,' he said. 'I ran into Miss Jendring when in pursuit of the thief, after Lady Alicia's diamonds had gone. And she said something like, "*But you do not think she is down here?*" She. She said "she", and I had not at that point informed her as to the probable gender of the thief.'

'Ah! She was speaking, then, of herself, or of one of her sisters.'

'I believe so.' Ballantine got to his feet, and waited, just for a moment, while his head pounded afresh and his stomach heaved. Damn and blast it, he was not yet ready for this.

Gussie gently took his arm, and steadied him. 'There, now. Do not hurry yourself overmuch.'

'Miss Werth, this unlooked-for solicitude is making me very nervous. I pray you will abandon it, and return to your customary mockery.'

'Doubtless I shall, soon enough.'

'I should prefer you to do so immediately, if you please.'

'Oh, very well.' Gussie dropped his arm, and stepped away from him, and he felt that he could once again breathe. He did so, deeply, and then sighed.

'Now for it, then. An unpleasant scene is likely, I'm afraid, but I suppose it is of no use encouraging you to absent yourself from it.'

'Having done so much work to apprehend this thief, nothing could prevent me from attending her capture.'

'Work! Do you call it that? You dabbled, Miss Werth, and were more hindrance than help.'

'You are very welcome, Mr. Ballantine.' Undaunted, Gussie dimpled into a smile, and curtseyed.

That was the worst of Gussie: even at her most maddening, he was sometimes hard-pressed not to smile back. 'Hmph. Come along, then.'

He had not got much beyond the door, though, before Theo appeared, moving in some haste. 'Ah! Ballantine. Glad I've got you.'

He ignored Gussie, who took this amiss. 'Good morning, *cousin,*' she said, with another smile, but not the pleasant kind she had been directing at Ballantine.

'Gussie.' Theo, oblivious, nodded. 'I was down in the kitchens, and I overheard something that may prove pertinent.'

'Gossip, Theo? How unlike you.'

'That being so,' interrupted Ballantine, before Gussie could rile the man, 'I imagine it is worth hearing, no?'

Annoyance flickered over Theo's face, and was gone. 'The kitchen maids. They said Fanny Jendring sent back her sister's breakfast, so they gave it to me instead. Wyrde is, um. The moving of objects without touching them. Possibly without needing to see them, though I don't know about that.'

'For example, jewellery,' said Gussie.

Theo nodded at her. 'Perhaps.'

Gussie looked at Ballantine. 'It all fits, doesn't it?'

'Yes, and very neatly.'

Gussie beamed.

'Yet, I must advise caution,' continued Ballantine. 'Sometimes a neat picture can still be missing a few pieces.'

'Well, the best way to be sure must be to interrogate the Jendrings.'

'And so we shall. Lord Bedgberry, do you join us?'

'I should only be in the way.' Theo rolled his shoulders, and shook himself. 'Besides, I want to play.'

'Oh, no.' Gussie sighed. 'Only try not to be too discordant, Theo, if you please? It makes my head ache.'

'Do not seek to direct the course of art, cousin.' Theo directed at her a very severe stare, then turned without further remark and left.

'Theo, turned artistic and moody,' Gussie remarked. 'Who would have thought it.'

'There is some precedent for the moods, I think.'

'And now he has an excuse for them.' It was not very long before the first notes of the organ sounded in the distance, and Gussie permitted herself a short sigh, massaging her temples. Ballantine sympathised: his aching head pulsed in time with every resounding chord. 'I could wish he had developed a passion for something less – thunderous,' Gussie sighed. 'The flute, perhaps.'

'There is still time. Soon he shall be removed from proximity to the organ. You might, perhaps, purchase him a flute, and hope for the best.'

'I shall! Or a harp. How charmingly he would play.'

Ballantine smiled. 'Well, but shall we go? There is yet time to question the Jendrings before the ball begins.'

Gussie studied him in momentary thought, and did not immediately answer.

'Well?' he prompted.

'And were you planning to dance, Mr. Ballantine?'

He blinked, taken aback by the abrupt change in subject. 'I was not.'

'Ah,' said Gussie. 'Very proper, I am sure. An absurd pursuit, all frivolity.'

'Were *you* planning to dance?'

'I had quite set my heart on it, yes.' She strode to the door and, with her customary decisiveness, threw it open. 'The Jendrings' quarters are this way.'

Ballantine followed, meekly enough, in Gussie's train as she swept down the hallway. She really was a queen of a woman, dauntless and focused, unstoppable when she put her mind to something. Useless to try to contain a force of nature; he would as well order a hurricane to cease and desist.

'Miss Jendring!' called she, shortly afterwards, paused in front of a stoutly closed door, and pounded upon it in a most forth-right manner. 'A word, if you please ma'am.'

Silence.

Gussie knocked again – more loudly, somehow, than before. She waited with visible impatience.

Ballantine stood like a rock, immoveable. He felt a growing sense of certainty, though he could not have said why: nobody was going to answer the door.

'We are too late, I think,' he suggested.

Gussie glanced back at him. A touch, and the handle twisted under her fingers: she opened the door, and slipped inside.

Ballantine, though, found himself arrested before he could follow. 'You are seeking the Jendrings?' somebody said, from directly behind him.

He jumped, and turned. Close by stood by far the most ancient person he had ever beheld. She resembled a sack of ancient leather, withered and dry, with two bright eyes in her wizened face, and a lace-trimmed gown of surpassing loveliness hung about her thin frame. 'I do, ma'am,' said he, offering her a bow. 'Do you happen to know where I might find them?'

'You would be fortunate to find any trace of them now.' The lady laughed, in a fashion rather odd. There was a too-bright sheen to her eyes, which Ballantine could not at all account for, and she seemed out of breath.

'Mr. Ballantine?' Gussie's face appeared around the door. 'Are you coming—Oh! Mrs. Fortescue. Excellent. Perhaps you can tell us where to find the Jendrings?'

Mary Fortescue. Ballantine took a closer, harder look at the woman – and at her attire. Her gown was pure silk, every inch of it, and a sumptuous deep blue hue; costly lace adorned the neck and the cuffs. What's more, she wore a sapphire brooch at her throat.

Nothing to cavil at in that: a woman may be elderly, but that did not oblige her to abandon all that was costly or beautiful in her garb.

Nonetheless, something about her appearance did not fit. Perhaps it was her hair: disorganised, as lady's coiffures went. Clearly she had not enjoyed the assistance of a lady's maid.

'How beautiful a brooch, ma'am,' he said, smiling. 'Where did you come by it?'

Mary Fortescue took a step back. 'A gift, from my daughter...'

'How very obliging of her.' Gussie stepped out of the Jendrings' rooms, and turned her attention upon the hapless Mary. 'A princely gift, to be sure.'

'Yes, she did very well for herself.' Mary took another step back, and another.

'And the gown?' said Ballantine.

Mary set her lips tightly, refusing to answer.

'Did you, by chance, get it from Mrs. Jendring?' he pursued. 'Or one of the other Jendring ladies?'

'I do not know why you should think so,' said Mary, firmly enough, but her eyes darted sideways. Seeking an escape?

Gussie anticipated the same, for she moved at once to place herself in the woman's path. 'Now that you mention it, Mr. Ballantine, I do believe I saw Mrs. Jendring in this very gown two nights ago.'

'That is what I thought.' Ballantine stared hard at the ancient face, watching as it slowly paled. 'Come now, ma'am. Tell us what you know of the Jendrings' departure, at the very least.'

'*One* is gone into the Dreaming, and the rest are – gone elsewhere.' Something calmed Mary with the words, for she stood straighter, firmer, and returned Ballantine's gaze without fear.

'What might "the Dreaming" be, and where could they possibly have gone?'

'They might have somehow stolen the Lord's carriage,' Gussie put in. 'But I cannot think how. We have not seen any trace of it since we arrived.'

'Have not either one of you entered the Dreaming, yet?' said Mary, in an odd, singsong voice. 'Perhaps your turn will come, this night.'

Ballantine exchanged a look with Gussie. Some thought struck her; she disappeared into the Jendrings' suite, and shortly afterwards reappeared again.

'Fanny Jendring,' she said. 'She is laid out on her bed.'

Dead, then – after the odd fashion that prevailed about the palace.

'She Dreams deeply,' said Mary, blithely. 'Who can say of what? Some, they do not return. But the young have reasons enough.'

'Is that what took Frosty?' asked Gussie. 'And Lord Maundevyle?'

'And the eldest Miss Jendring,' said Ballantine. 'But all returned.'

'As will this one.' Mary Fortescue nodded wisely.

Gussie paced a step or two. 'Is that what you meant when you said the other Jendrings are gone? Are their corpses to be found somewhere about the place?'

Ballantine shook his head, reading a denial on Mary's wizened face, though she said no more. 'They are gone from the palace, and I may be wrong, but I believe they have taken Lady Alicia's diamonds with them.'

'They left Fanny here?' Gussie seemed horrified. 'But she is defenceless.'

Mary cackled, a harsh sound ending in a bout of coughing. 'Defenceless! Not that one.'

Ballantine frowned. She could move objects about at will, and from a distance; to be sure, that could be turned to all manner of uses. But Mary's vehemence struck a strange note with him.

'Have you had occasion to put her defensive capabilities to the test?' asked Gussie, her train of thought following his.

Mary grinned, displaying a mouthful of blackened and broken teeth. 'Almost killed me, she did. Pity.'

'Almost killed—nothing can kill you.' Gussie frowned, her troubled gaze searching Mary's face. 'Though... Goodspeed performed a change-about with the Wyrde. For a while, you were not immortal, were you?'

'But why should Fanny Jendring attack you?' put in Ballantine. 'Come ma'am, time is wasting. I should be much obliged if you would cease these games, and be frank.'

Mary fingered the sapphire brooch at her throat, her thin frame swaying dreamily. 'And what brought you in search of the ladies Jendring tonight?' she countered. 'Thought them thieves, did you?'

'Are not they?' said Gussie.

'Fanny, at the least,' put in Ballantine. 'Yet you are wearing a gown of her mother's. Did you catch them at it, ma'am? This finery of yours is the price of your silence, perhaps.'

Mary began to cackle again, and to cough, paroxysms of both that left her shaking. 'Ah, I have not enjoyed a conversation so much in years,' she choked. 'What fools, the young!'

'Oh,' said Gussie. 'Oh, Hugh, we have got it all wrong.'

'So I gather, but I do not see how,' answered Ballantine, his attention caught, briefly, by her use of his name.

'It was *you* thieving jewels.' Gussie jabbed a finger at Mary Fortescue. 'And I do not know why, but a woman with hundreds of years behind her may have different ideas of morality to the rest of us.'

Enlightenment dawned: several missing pieces clicked together at once. 'And Fanny Jendring caught *you* with the jewels. That is why she attacked you?'

'Miss Jendring the elder knew days ago, however,' said Gussie, shaking her head at him. 'She knew who you were chasing, the night of the mummery, and did not choose to assist you. Why didn't she?'

Ballantine thought quickly. 'Miss Jendring saw you steal something,' he hazarded. 'That first night at the palace. They are no wealthy family; perhaps she had thoughts of apprehending you herself, in hope of a reward. Or perhaps she even had thoughts of forcing you to share.'

Annoyance flickered over Mary's face. 'Such fools, the young,' she said again. 'Oughtn't tangle with me.'

Gussie advanced upon the old woman. 'Fanny discovered your hoard and took it, did not she? That is what you meant by your warning at Misrule.'

'All that glitters is not gold,' Ballantine quoted. 'You referred to yourself there, I suppose.'

'*She who risks all for finery will rue and rue again,*' Gussie added. 'Did Fanny attack you, or was it the other way about?'

'I had a fancy,' Mary crooned. 'To enjoy myself, just this one last night. And why should I not?'

This made no sense to Ballantine, or to Gussie either: they stared, puzzled, at the serene face of Mary Fortescue.

The Jendrings were gone, but Mary was still here. Where were the jewels?

'Who has the diamonds, ma'am?' Ballantine pressed.

'Ah, well,' sighed Mary. A sudden movement caught Ballantine's eye: so slight a shift of her hand, it could almost be nothing at all – were it not for the bloom of blood, vivid and shocking.

With a soundless sigh, the ancient, dauntless old woman slumped slowly backwards, and fell against the wall.

'What the—' Ballantine stuttered, and lunged. He was on his knees beside her in an instant, helpless to assist: the weapon was only a hatpin, but the damage it inflicted was well targeted. Blood flowed, stealing Mary Fortescue's life away with it.

Gussie stood at a distance, frozen with horror – or perhaps dawning realisation. 'Theo said Fanny returned her sister's breakfast, and they gave it to him. Blood, then. Miss Jendring is like Theo, is not she? Why then did she not want her breakfast?'

'Either she acquired a meal elsewhere,' said Ballantine grimly. 'Or she was changed about with someone else's Wyrde, and no longer wanted it.'

'Goodspeed never changed the two of you back, did he?' Gussie approached at last, and sat by Mary's side with a sigh. 'She has got your Wyrde, and you have got hers.'

'Which means,' Ballantine added gently, 'you can die. At last.'

Mary was fading fast, but life enough remained in her to chuckle, wetly. 'I warned her. Sounds jolly enough now, I daresay, but someday—'

She never finished the sentence, for the light died out of her eyes: she was gone.

How quickly the centuries caught up with her, once the animating force of her was gone. Her face seemed, in an instant, shrivelled almost beyond recognition, her skin shrunken, her body skeletal-thin.

Ballantine and Gussie sat in shocked silence for a time, both, perhaps, occupied with their own dark reflections at so unexpected a scene.

Gussie broke it at last. 'I have to say that I do not altogether blame her. *I* should not at all like to live forever.'

'Nor I,' Ballantine agreed. 'Though I wish she had not felt it necessary to – expedite her own passing.'

'Do you feel responsible?'

Ballantine tore his eyes from Mrs. Fortescue's dead face, and frowned at Gussie. 'We pressed her too hard.'

'She *was* a thief. That is your duty, is not it?'

'It is,' he sighed. 'But it does not usually end in so sad an outcome.'

'It is the outcome she wanted.'

'Yes,' he agreed. 'That is what's sad about it.'

'The Wyrde is never kind.' Gussie rose to her feet, and shook out her skirts.

'Neither is the law.'

Gussie studied him as he hauled himself upright, conscious anew of the pain in his head. 'You, however, are,' she told him.

'I am what?'

'Kind. Always.'

He scowled. 'I have neither time nor patience for your nonsense, Miss Werth. A woman is dead, a pack of either blackmailers or thieves or both are missing, and my head aches dreadfully.'

'Yes, I wonder how the Jendrings contrived to vanish?' she mused, ignoring the rest. 'Perhaps Fanny will know.'

'Aye, pity that she is dead. Or whatever the state should be called.'

'Isn't it?' Gussie smiled at him with a degree of cheer he considered highly unpromising, and strode back to the half-open door of the Jendrings' erstwhile suite. 'I daresay there is something to be done about it, however,' she declared, and vanished inside.

Briefly, Ballantine considered leaving her to it. With a groan, he mastered this unworthy impulse, and staggered after her.

Distantly, he realised that the soaring symphony of Theo's organ music had ceased.

CHAPTER SEVENTEEN

Lassitude struck Theo without warning, so swiftly he had no time even to wonder about it.

He *had* been engaged in a riotous rendition of Beethoven's fifth symphony, and what grand, shattering splendour it had been. The crescendo beckoned; Theo poured his soul into every note, swept away by the drama of it, the exquisite harmony—

—His fingers slipped, a harsh discordancy blossomed like a bruise—

—The symphony ended between one breath and the next, and in fact, that next breath never arrived at all. Anybody passing would have discovered the inert form of Lord Bedgberry slumped over the silent organ, his face frozen in an expression of mixed startlement and fury.

Nobody did, however. Many of those left yet alert, unclaimed by the thing called the Dreaming, may have noticed the abrupt cessation of Theo's jangling symphony, and blessed their lucky stars for the silence (most of them being in no better state than Mr. Ballantine, as far as over indulgence went).

Where did Theo go, after this inelegant and impromptu demise? For while his body existed in a stasis near indistinguishable from death, his mind roamed unencumbered, lost in the deepest of dreams.

The deepest and also the strangest of dreams, for the greater part of his life passed again behind his mind's eye, yet all the details twisted themselves about. He spent a long time wandering the passages of Werth Towers all over again, his deeds (and that of his family) stranger and more terrible than ever they had been in life. He relived the fire that had claimed so much of the old estate; Lord Felix's final demise, and every atrocity the old lord had committed before that happy event; Aunt Wheldrake and her storms of passion or rage; a swarm of departed spirits, ordinarily visible only to Nell, but now free to torment him as they chose; and, of course, every single one of Gussie's more hair-raising antics in livid detail.

His dreams caught on the angelic countenance of the duplicitous Mrs. Daughtry, and there remained for some time. Theo was obliged to relive every humiliating moment of her manipulation of him, the ease with which she had mesmerised and controlled him, how near she had come to the destruction of his family with her avarice.

It was somewhere in the midst of this that a species of consciousness returned. How unlike him, to dwell on memories he did not enjoy! For what was the use of torturing himself over things that had already happened, and were gone forever? Most impractical. Why, then, was he wallowing in all this now?

The dream slowed around him, Mrs. Daughtry paused in the process of attempting to abscond. Everything took on a blurred unreality, as though he beheld the events from behind a film of running water; and a soft voice spoke, dulcet and creeping, whispering in his very ear with a repulsive semblance of intimacy.

'If you had come with me willingly, all this might have been different.'

For a panicked moment, Theo thought it Mrs. Daughtry's voice he heard, and imagined her returned to torment him afresh.

But, no. Those deep, velvety tones were not hers. He had heard them recently: where...

Ah.

'Your majesty, I presume,' he sighed.

She laughed. 'A lively intellect. No wonder your dreams are so deliciously clear.'

'And what are you doing rummaging through them, like a chest full of old clothes?'

'A remarkably perspicacious insight. I am – borrowing ideas, much the same way I might borrow an old gown.'

'And what do you propose to do with them?'

'Where do you imagine all my fine glamours come from?' she countered. 'I cannot quite dream them up out of nothing, you know. I must have material.'

'You are the Lady of this house,' he realised. 'And all its wonders are yours.'

'Many of them,' she agreed. 'And if you come here ready to enjoy my efforts, why should not you all pay for them?'

'These are private dreams! I don't like you riffling through them, like a book left lying around for just anybody to pick up.'

'And what were you doing with them that is so important? You do not even like these dreams. I can feel the disgust in you. Let me have them, then. I will turn them to good account, I promise you.'

'Oh, take whatever you like, and go away,' growled Theo. 'I want to get back to my playing.'

'Marvellous,' the Lady crowed. He felt *combed*, as though a net were drawn through the deep waters of his mind.

When the sight returned to his staring eyes, he discovered himself to have fallen face-first into the polished oak of his beloved organ. His back ached like the Devil when he straightened, and as he set his stiffened fingers to the keys once more they were, at first, wretchedly clumsy.

'A pox on all of you,' he muttered, meaning the Lady for certain, and likely Mrs. Daughtry as well, though fewer recollections of her now troubled him than had done so before.

The music that next poured forth from the deep spaces in his soul proved to be a funeral dirge. Considering the state in which he had spent the previous few hours, Theo considered this fitting enough.

GUSSIE'S ATTEMPTS TO REVIVE Fanny Jendring were well enough, in themselves. She shouted her name several times over, her own face pushed up close to the young lady's, so as to maximise the chances of her hearing it. She grasped the girl's shoulders and shook her like a dusty carpet. She uttered one or two choice insults, in hope of enraging her back to alertness, and Ballantine helpfully added a threat of his own (on the subject of thieving and the penalties for it, which ought to be enough to horrify anybody of ordinary sensibility).

Really, she put a lot of effort into the endeavour; it could hardly be considered her fault that none of it worked.

'Very well then,' she declared at last, rising from the bedside of the deceased young person. 'Whatever this "Dreaming" is, it appears to have an inflexible hold upon her. We shall have to think of something else.'

'Such as?' Ballantine did not move from the chair he had taken by the window, having held no high opinion of Gussie's chances of success – a fact he had made patent enough, with his sceptical remarks and his grave looks. He was not very amusing when he was sad, and his head ached, facts which Gussie considered it sensible to remember in the future. A contented Mr. Ballantine enjoying good health tended to suit her purposes much better.

'I don't know, exactly,' Gussie admitted, and began a fresh quest about the Jendrings' chambers. She had already conducted a hasty sweep of the rooms, but at that time she had been looking for signs of life or ongoing habitation. Now, she moved more slowly through the suite, paying much closer attention to details which had escaped her before.

The Jendrings were housed in comfort, if not in splendour. Three bedchambers adjoined one another, each upholstered in attractive shades of blue. Their parlour bore cheerful wainscotting and a quantity of comfortable furnishings, long windows offering a view of a star-spangled midnight sky. An air of disorganisation reigned: the ladies were not of neat habits, it seemed. Cushions pulled off the chairs lay on the floor, and someone's embroidery had been left behind in a heap near the hearth. One or two discarded books lay scattered about, two set in a stack beside a low divan, and another lying open upon a windowsill.

Gussie swept through each bedchamber in turn, peeking into the closets (empty) and casting a suspicious eye under the beds (likewise). Fanny Jendring lay still in the farthest of these, still as motionless as a felled tree; Ballantine sat still by the window, almost as inert.

'Well?' said he, rather wearily, as she returned into the room.

'Nothing of use or note.'

'We do seem to be stymied, then. I suppose I can look into whether or not one of those carriages was accessible to them, but if it was, they could be anywhere by now.'

'Surely they are gone back to their London home?'

'If so, they will be gone from it again before we are like to get there.'

'This seems very defeatist, Mr. Ballantine. Have you no zeal for thief-taking today?'

'Perhaps I simply know when I am beaten.' He let the statement stand for several moments, then slowly stood up, and stretched. 'No, you are right. It has been so strange a few days as to addle my wits, I fear.'

Gussie stood frowning down at Fanny Jendring's still face. 'I wonder if it is her embroidery lying abandoned in the parlour. If so, she is not very good at it. And the books...'

Hmm. The books. There had been nothing remarkable about any of them, at a glance: such featureless things she had taken little note of them. But a dedicated investigator examined everything, did not they? However innocuous they may seem.

'I will return momentarily,' Gussie told Ballantine. She was gone in an instant, ignoring the look of puzzled enquiry he directed at her.

Moments passed, and then many more, and she did not return.

BALLANTINE WITNESSED GUSSIE SAIL out of the room again, relentless in the pursuit of whatever it was she had bethought herself of. He devoted himself to an investigation of his own, scrutinising Miss Fanny Jendring more closely than he had before, and conducting a thorough search of her room. He made his way through each of the other two bedchambers after that, and finally arrived in the parlour.

Fully five more minutes passed, and so intent was he upon his study of the Jendrings' few remaining possessions, he was disgracefully slow to realise one very significant point: Gussie was not in the room.

'Miss Werth?' he called.

No answer came. He looked at his watch, frowning. How long had it been since she had left Fanny's side, promising to return any moment? At least twenty minutes, perhaps more.

She had left their apartments, then, and gone off on some fresh errand of her own. How odd of her, though, to do so in the midst of an investigation. She had gone to check something, or fetch something, that pertained in some way to the Jendrings' absence; that must be it.

But another twenty minutes passed, and she did not come back. Despite himself – despite his knowledge of Gussie's capability – his unease grew from a faint prickle at the back of his mind to an unmanageable beast, roaring with disquiet no matter how he tried to concentrate on something else.

'Wretched woman,' he muttered, and with a long sigh he abandoned his search of the Jendrings' rooms, and set off on a search for Gussie instead.

He did not find her. Not by the side of poor Mary Fortescue; not in her own rooms with her family; not in the breakfast parlours or the dining-room or the ballrooms. He found her nowhere, and no one he enquired with had seen her for some time.

He ended up at last at the organ, where Theo still thundered away at his Beethoven. 'Lord Bedgberry!' he bellowed, and shook the man by the shoulder.

'What?' Theo turned about, his face as thunderous as his abandoned music.

'Gussie is missing.'

'And what is there in that to trouble you? May none of us have a moment's peace?'

'If you imagine she is merely gone away with a headache, or something of the sort, you are mistaken. She was investigating. With me.'

'And you went and lost her, did you? I call that damned careless.'

'It was, I admit. But I am concerned, and I beg you to put your mind to the problem of what may have become of her.'

'How should I know? If you think I have any better notion what goes on in Gussie's head than you do, you're a fool.'

Cursing, Ballantine abandoned Lord Bedgberry, and returned to the last place he had seen her: the Jendrings' parlour. He stood in the centre of the deserted chamber, helpless and worried and livid with anger at himself. He knew her propensity for getting into trouble: how could he have taken his eyes off her, even for a moment?

Footsteps sounded in the passage, moving quickly: Ballantine's heart leapt.

But it was Lord Bedgberry coming in, visibly out of temper. 'Well? Have you found her?'

'No.'

His lordship gave his cravat an irritable tug. 'Devil take it, Gussie, what have you gone and done now—' He stopped short.

Ballantine followed the line of his gaze. The window. Lord Bedgberry was staring out of the window. She could not possibly have gone out of it, could she? If so, she had carefully closed it again behind herself; not likely.

But Theo paid no attention to the window. He stalked over to it, and stood staring down at a pair of books lying open upon the window-sill.

'She has left her journal here,' he said. 'Now, why would she have done that?'

'Miss Werth keeps a journal?' Ballantine went over to the window, intent on examining the thing, but Lord Bedgberry put out an arm, preventing him.

'Don't touch it.'

'Whyever not?'

'Because something strange is afoot, that's why not. Do you not recall where you are?' He fished in a pocket of his own, and brought out another journal: a red-bound one. He waved this at Ballantine, much to the Runner's puzzlement. 'We knew there were two of these. Now, it appears, there are at least three.'

'You aren't making sense, man,' said Ballantine in frustration. 'Three journals? I daresay there are far more than three of those in the world.'

'These are no ordinary journals. They move about some-times, although there is no catching them at it. And it is damned difficult to ignore them: if you don't write in them for a while, there's no peace until you do. Dashed importunate things. I do not think Gussie has left hers out of her possession since she got it, and yet here it lies.'

Ballantine stared down at the little book, inoffensive as it seemed. One of the pages had some writing on it, scrawled in a careless hand: he bent over the book, struggling to make out what it said.

Like calls to like: book calls to book. I beseech you, show me what became of the Misses Jendring.

He glanced at Theo, but the man looked no more enlightened than he was himself.

'Very well then,' said Theo, and took up a pen. He set his own journal open on the window-sill beside Gussie's, and the other, unidentified one, and wrote hastily.

Like calls to like: book calls to book. I beseech you, show me what became of Augusta Werth.

Nothing happened immediately. Ballantine and Theo stood in expectant silence, conscious of every slightest sound or flicker of movement.

A page rustled: a soft, crisp sound.

Then, the book *opened*.

Oh, it had been open before, its pages splayed wide for the perusal of its contents. But something else opened within it, something cavernous, depthless: the covers yawned wider and wider and a dark heart beckoned within.

'Right then,' said Theo, pushing up his sleeves. Before Ballantine could stop him – before he could even grasp what his lordship intended to do – Theo had taken those two flimsy covers in a grip of steel and engaged himself in wrenching them further apart.

The cavern expanded, opened up into a musty-smelling passage thick with dust. From somewhere deep within, Ballantine caught the faint chatter of feminine voices.

Theo's brows rose. 'Excellent,' said he, and, in a single, impossible step, he was off down the passage, his shoes kicking up quantities of grime that came billowing out from between the pages.

The covers, Ballantine noticed with horror, were inexorably closing again. He had only moments to decide whether to follow—

—He could not leave Lord Bedgberry to field, potentially, some four or five forthright women at once; there might be social obligations. Etiquette. Tea parties—

—He took the step before he had time to talk himself out of it, and felt the world lurch, sickeningly, around him.

Then the wainscot of the parlour vanished in favour of something crisper, dustier, lighter – walls, Ballantine realised, not only covered with paper but made out of it, a thick parchment creased and stained with the patina of time.

The floor underfoot was parchment, too, and it swayed as he traversed it. A disconcerting experience; his stomach heaved in protest.

The passage opened out into an expansive chamber, high-ceilinged and airy. The dust was not so chokingly thick here: someone had been cleaning, he judged.

No furniture occupied the chamber, but a large carpet lay in the centre of the floor, a vibrant thing woven in many colours. Seated around its edges with their gowns spread out like petals were: two young Jendring ladies, their mother, their aunt, and Gussie.

Lord Bedgberry stood glaring down at the lot of them, fair snarling with disgust. 'Here I have been sent on an urgent mission to find you – poor Ballantine out of his wits with worry – and you are engaged in nothing more dangerous than a gossiping party!'

'I should have thought neither of you could imagine me to be in any danger,' Gussie said with sparkling reproach, though the look she cast at *Ballantine* when he came up to them held a question in it.

'I was concerned,' said Ballantine quietly, in answer.

'Have I been gone so very long?'

'Near two hours, I reckon.'

'I should have come out again in another half-hour. My business here is nearly concluded.'

'And what, precisely, is your business here?' Ballantine turned his attention to the Jendring ladies: the two elder watching him with some wariness; Miss Jendring going to some trouble to appear unconcerned; and Miss Cecily looking shame-faced.

'I believe we are arriving at an agreement with regards to the problem of the jewellery.'

'It was all a freak of Antonia's,' declared Cecily. 'And Fanny's! *I* do not care half so much for finery, I assure you.'

Miss Jendring sighed. 'You are not yet *quite* old enough to understand the necessity of being well-turned out if one wishes to be accepted in London, and the impossibility of being so without significant funds.'

Ballantine frowned at her. 'And you do not appear to be quite old enough to understand the severe unwisdom of stealing, Miss Jendring. Do not you know that you could hang for it?'

'It was reckless of me at first, I admit,' said she, cheerfully. 'But no power could hang me *now*, and so it all turns out for the best.'

'You mean you have got Mrs. Fortescue's Wyrde.'

Miss Jendring beamed. 'So liberating.'

'And have adopted her habits with it, it seems. I would advise you to reconsider.'

'Yes, our dear Miss Werth has been saying much the same thing.'

Ballantine turned a suspicious eye upon Gussie, who endeavoured to look very responsible. To his surprise, her left eyelid flickered in a wink.

'She has behaved shockingly,' said Mrs. Jendring. 'As has Fanny, and they are both in a great deal of trouble, Mr. Ballantine, I assure you.'

'Well, but we did not *steal* anything,' Miss Jendring protested. 'Mary did all that.'

'You bartered them off her in exchange for your Wyrde, did you?' Ballantine guessed. 'So that she could fulfil her long-held wish of departing that lengthy life of hers.'

'She was only too glad to let me have them. And dear Goodspeed only too happy to help.'

Gussie frowned. 'I hope he did not know about the jewellery.'

'You cannot imagine me such a fool as to tell him about *that*.' Miss Jendring seemed offended by the suggestion.

Ballantine sighed. 'Receiving stolen property is little better than stealing it yourself, Miss Jendring. Especially if you knew it to be stolen.'

She wilted a little at that. 'Then how are we to afford gowns for our season? And where are we to get the jewels to wear with them? Even debutantes are covered head to toe in diamonds and pearls, these days.'

'It is not that I fail to sympathise with your plight,' Ballantine said, in a tone devoid of any sympathy whatsoever. 'But this scheme of yours won't answer.'

'The poor things have been hiding in here for some time,' said Gussie. 'What a terrible mess it has all got into! But we are arriving at a resolution between us.'

'Oh?' said Theo dangerously. 'And what might that be?'

'Why, if Miss Jendring would like to borrow my pearls, she need not purloin them: she need only ask. And so I have said.' Gussie beamed. 'I am sure my aunt will not at all mind lending some of her jewels either, and then there is only the gowns to be considered. I shall be sending them to Madame Fleur with the strongest recommendation to fit them out very handsomely. And there! No further need to bother with Lady Alicia's diamonds. They shall all be returned.'

Theo shook his head. 'I had thought it beyond even you to befriend a pack of reprobates, Gussie, but it seems I am mistaken.'

'How ungenerous! When you are as great a reprobate as any of them, in your own way.'

Theo opened his mouth, on the point of uttering some blistering retort: then, thinking better of it, shut it again, the words unsaid. He turned instead, and stalked back up the papery passageway towards the exit.

'And my part in this is to pretend I know nothing of the Misses Jendrings' interference in Mary Fortescue's thieving?' Ballantine said.

'No, you are to do one better. Without the Miss Jendrings' *interference,* as you put it, we may not have discovered the culprit at all. Therefore, if there is a reward to be offered for the return of the jewels, it is to be paid to them, if you please. I imagine Lady Alicia can be persuaded to be generous.'

Ballantine blinked, incredulity temporarily rendering him speechless. 'And what of justice?' he managed at last. 'What of the law?'

'The law is too vast and sprawling a creature to bother herself over a few women wanting handsomer attire. And the true culprit has got her heart's desire, putting her, in the same step, beyond the reach of justice. And justice, I may as well add, is very cruel indeed, if it proposes to hang a person merely for purloining a few jewels.'

'A fortune in diamonds, emeralds and pearls! Do you not have any notion what such things are worth?'

'A woman's life?' Gussie fixed him with a level stare.

He found that he could not return it; he dropped his gaze. 'I admit that your solution is rather neat,' he allowed.

Gussie, taking this for a ringing endorsement, clapped her hands with satisfaction. 'Then we are all agreed. Shall we, then, get out of this odd place, and return to the palace? The ball will be in progress already, I suppose, and I am wild for dancing.'

Ballantine stared at her in undisguised wonder. She had solved a crime, witnessed a woman's death, uncovered the oddest room in existence bound up in the heart of a pocket-book, and neatly rearranged the lives of some four or five people, to boot. After all of which, all she could think of was dancing?

'What about this – book?' he asked, waving an arm, vaguely, at the paper-crisp space around them.

'Oh, yes. Antonia has a journal just like mine and Theo's, is not that remarkable? She got it in a parcel, as I did, and has no more notion of the sender than we do. Was not it clever of her to discover this room in it? I would never have thought of such a thing.'

'Did you create this room, Miss Jendring?'

She shook her head. 'I have not such power, Mr. Ballantine. I do not know who has.'

He sighed. One mystery yet remained, then: just who had sent those journals to Gussie, Theo and Antonia? And what was the nature of this strange room, to which all three books seemingly connected?

'I am too tired for any more mysteries today,' Gussie announced, punctuating her statement with a yawn. 'I only want to dance, and drink punch, and gossip.' She rose to her feet, drawing Miss Jendring with her. 'Come, let us dress, and away to the ball! Mr. Ballantine, will you be so good as to assist with their luggage?'

Several portmanteaus lay scattered about, he now saw: the ladies had been sitting on them. 'You were hoping there would be another way out of here, I collect.'

'Yes, we were staging a daring escape,' answered Miss Jendring. 'What a pity we were foiled.'

'But it is not, for now you shall still go to the Masquerade, and so shall I.' Gussie abandoned Ballantine to the shepherding of the luggage and two middle-aged ladies, waltzing away with her arm through Miss Jendring's, and Miss Cecily trailing after.

'I must introduce you to Clarissa,' Ballantine heard her saying as the group disappeared from view. 'I do believe you will adore each other.'

CHAPTER EIGHTEEN

WHATEVER THE PECULIARITIES OF the first few days at the palace might have been, the Masquerade Ball was all that it ought to be.

Gussie presented herself in a sumptuous violet domino and matching mask, her gown a deep indigo blue, and sewn from silk that rustled delightfully when she moved. She felt dark and dramatic, and very striking, the glances of many gentlemen supporting her in the belief that she looked very well indeed.

She did not lack for partners, but neither did anybody else. The whole company proved as wild for dancing as Gussie was herself, and no wonder: *here* was the grand event they had all anticipated, here the waltzes, the mystique, the flirting and drinking, the merriment and mirth of civilised entertainment. The Grand Masquerade for the Wyrde – and Wondrous! At last! And wondrous it was.

The Lord and Lady caused a stir, when at last they appeared, together, at the opening of the ball. Both so handsome! And so rich! Why, anybody could tell they were rich just to look at them, their attire everything that was sumptuous and costly, and their house! Well. Even a duke had not near so many rooms.

Just who they might be behind their elegant black masks, nobody could guess. Not for a lack of trying; for half the night, every snippet of conversation Gussie overheard consisted of some fevered speculation as to their identities: *royalty of some sort,* was heard several times, and: *it is not* said *to be possible, but really I should not wonder if they did not possess two or three shades of Wyrde apiece.*

For herself, Gussie's curiosity on the subject could not wholly absorb her. She was too happy: in her succession of partners and the liveliness of the dancing; in the glasses of punch, fresh and delicious, of which she imbibed rather too many; in the company of her family, all of whom had presented themselves for the dance (even Theo, for some reason), and all of whom seemed resolved upon presenting a creditable appearance (even Great-Aunt Honoria, incredibly).

What was more, the strange affliction that had (seemingly) taken Frosty from the world had passed – from everyone. All those who had, for some time, lain in a death-like stupor rose from it in time for the Ball; and those who had imagined themselves bereaved were driven, by relief and a cessation of mourning, into fresh heights of gaiety. Miss Frostell, a little weakened by her long sojourn in that state, nonetheless came down to the ballroom for the masque, though Gussie ensured that she stationed herself in a comfortable chair, and did not seek to exert herself too much.

'I shall be very well, my dear,' insisted she, and so she continued to say, every time Gussie paused in her merriment long enough to check on her dearest friend (which, in credit to what passed for Gussie's heart, was fairly often).

Gussie danced with both the Selwyn brothers, and then with Clarissa (who, garbed once more in gentleman's accoutrements, declared herself an honorary man, and quite worthy to dance with all ladies – and all the men, as well, if she so chose). Gussie danced the waltz with Henry, then again with Mr. Portman; several cotillions with gentlemen whose names she could not, afterwards, remember; and country-dances beyond counting.

The one gentleman who refused, with maddening stubbornness, to honour her with his hand – or, the coward, to approach her at all – was Mr. Ballantine. Every time Gussie was at leisure, he seemed to be urgently occupied. After a while, she suspected him of doing it on purpose. He kept avoiding her eye.

Finally, when the hour grew late and some of the dancers began at last to retire, Gussie took matters into her own hands. Mr. Ballantine, lurking near the punch table, seemed engaged in earnest conversation with a red-haired young lady in a pale pink mask and gown; so absorbed by her remarks, in fact, as not to see Gussie as she approached (or so it *seemed*). But he was very aware of her, she thought: it cost a man a strong effort to avoid glancing at one part specific of the room for half an hour together.

'Mr. Ballantine,' she said, and performed a curtsey.

He looked at her at last, taking in the dramatic sweep of her domino and gown with a look of faint despair. 'Miss Werth.' He relented so far as to bow to her, though with evident reluctance. 'You are acquainted with Miss Turnbull, perhaps?'

'I am not, nor do I care to be.' Gussie smiled brilliantly upon the hapless Miss Turnbull, who withdrew in high dudgeon.

'That was very rude,' said Ballantine gravely.

'As has been your conduct, for you have been ignoring me all night.'

'I have merely been otherwise occupied.'

'For so many hours together?'

He was silent.

'It would not be improper for us to dance, if that concerns you. Really, we are scarcely related at all. I doubt we share more than two or three drops of familial blood.'

'That was not, in fact, my concern.'

'Then what is? Come, out with it, so we may be rid of it.'

'I had not planned to dance, Miss Werth, as I told you.'

'And I do not expect you to dance very much. Only the once, if you really cannot bear it.'

He looked at her face, silent in some unknowable thought. 'You are so eager to dance with me, are you?'

'It has become a point of principle.'

'Because I protested.'

'Yes, exactly.'

He smiled, faintly. 'You do not like to be denied anything you desire, I perceive. What puzzles me is why you should desire this particular entertainment. I am no dancer, and shall probably tread on your feet.'

'Call it my whim, and let that be an end to it. I am a strange, capricious creature, you know, given to these odd flights of fancy. It is of no use trying to talk me into better sense.' She held out her hand, and said, beseechingly, 'Please?'

Mr. Ballantine took her hand, bowed over it – and released it. 'No, Gussie,' he said quietly. 'You will find a far better partner than I, I am sure of it.'

With which words he walked away from her, leaving her standing alone.

'But I do not want a better partner,' said she, softly. 'I want a stern, disapproving ogre of a man, whether he treads on my feet or no.'

But Ballantine was out of hearing. In another moment he was gone from the ballroom altogether, retiring, probably to bed, where even Gussie could not further importune him.

Gussie sighed, feeling momentarily forlorn. Well, and why should she feel bereft? He was right, of course: she would find a better partner. A handsome, young one, with liveliness and wit, who would pay her compliments, and perform the intricate steps of the dance with vigour and expertise. The room was full of such gentlemen.

Shrugging off her disappointed feelings, Gussie lifted her chin, and went in search of a suitable victim.

May 3rd

And so, we are restored to London – flown back in, via those marvellous carriages, and deposited upon our own doorstep. How weary we were! Several days of revelry, mystery and the Wyrde are enough to exhaust even my relentless energy, so my aunt observed. She is quite right. I did not stir from my bed until noon yesterday, and it has taken me until today to take up this journal again.

Clarissa declares herself mad with envy, because she has not got one of her own. I have told her, of course, about the strange room at the heart of the book. She has made me promise to take her there, and I have undertaken to do so – but not yet. We are all of us in need of a little peace and quiet. Let that mystery lie uncovered for a little while longer, then.

Miss Jendring has already called on us, with both of her sisters, and her Mama. They are to go to Madame Fleur on Wednesday, and I have written them a note. Theo has called me a fool for proposing to lend her my pearls: 'And she a thieving wench!' he called her, rather unfairly, for she is not quite that, is she? And men never can understand the peculiar and pressing demands of womanhood: the misery of the marriage market, the necessity (for many of us) of navigating it with success, the impossibility of doing so without the proper plumage. I did think it right to just mention to Miss Jendring that Mr. Ballantine remains relentless in his desire to bring her to justice: just in case she should develop any ideas of absconding with my pearls. She says she is resolved to live a blameless existence henceforth, and I do think I almost believe her.

Theo has gone away to his own rooms. Indeed he has ceased to pretend that they do not exist (unaccountable of him as it was). My uncle may well be right: perhaps he will cease to belong to us here at the townhouse, and remove to his rooms entirely. I daresay he will enjoy his independence, and he need not worry about dining: an enviable freedom, perhaps. He has taken his journal with him, of course, declaring the books too odd to co-exist in the same house. Perhaps he is right. I wonder if he goes there, sometimes – to the room at the heart of the book, I mean. To a man so in love with solitude as Theo, the space would certainly appeal.

Although if the Miss Jendrings also possess a journal, others may do, too. Who else might one encounter, wandering those dusty corridors? The creator of the books, perhaps? I am resolved upon making some one or two forays back into the journal myself, soon enough, and then we will see what we shall see.

Goodspeed has abandoned his mischievous ways, and gone back to being our staid and sensible butler. I taxed him with the service he performed for poor Mary Fortescue, and he did not deny it. I wonder whose Wyrde he was channelling, for those hours as the Master of Misrule? The Lord's, I believe: it would make sense if that gentleman possessed this power of change-about, as I believe Theo called it. He changed his own Wyrde with Goodspeed's, for the space of that evening, and Goodspeed employed it to change about everyone else's. An interesting skill. I have never before heard of another person whose Wyrde impacts the Wyrde of others – if not quite in the way mine does, then it seems at least a related capacity.

Frosty has settled in well, and seems restored to her old self. As does Henry. They will neither of them speak much of what occurred while they lay in the semblance of death: only muttering something about "strange dreams" if pressed. Theo told me an odd tale of the Lady, and collapsing over the organ, and some strange dreams of his own, and a bit of nonsense about glamours. I could not make head nor tail of it.

Here I shall leave off, for today, for we are bidden to the Selwyns' for dinner. As though we had not all had carousing enough, for one season! I look forward to a very dull evening, with no surprises. No thefts or deaths, no mysteries, no antics, and definitely no pageants. Like Miss Jendring, I have resolved upon living a blameless existence henceforward: the stern eye of Mr. Ballantine seems to demand it of me.

Unlike Miss Jendring, I do not at all expect to prove equal to it.

ALSO BY CHARLOTTE E. ENGLISH

House of Werth:

Wyrde and Wayward

Wyrde and Wicked

Wyrde and Wild

Wyrde and Wondrous

Modern Magick:

The Road to Farringale

Toil and Trouble

The Striding Spire

The Fifth Britain

Royalty and Ruin

Magick and Misadventure

...and many more!

www.charlotteenglish.com

Made in United States
North Haven, CT
17 December 2022